DÉJÀ VU

The tall elephant grass cut his skin as he shoved through it, followed by three other tourists who came crashing into the foliage behind him as they all attempted to escape the gunmen on the ridge.

Dan stepped around the brush and was startled to see that a long trench had been dug into the hillside. He ran along its edge for a short distance and then came to a halt when a soldier with a rusty rifle leaped out of the brush in front of him, a long, wicked bayonet pointed directly at him and his wife.

The soldier spoke, and even though Dan couldn't understand what he said, his actions warned the Americans to stop.

Dan's mouth gaped open when he recognized the crudely woven uniform and the rifle the Japanese soldier carried. At first the American felt disoriented and then realized where his sense of déjà vu was coming from: he'd seen soldiers like this one in the Pacific before.

But that was during World War II.

HarperPaperbacks by
Duncan Long

NIGHT STALKERS
GRIM REAPER
TWILIGHT JUSTICE
DESERT WIND
SEA WOLF
SHINING PATH
NEPTUNE THUNDER
BUDDHA'S CROWN

ATTENTION: ORGANIZATIONS AND CORPORATIONS

Most HarperPaperbacks are available at special quantity discounts for bulk purchases for sales promotions, premiums, or fund-raising. For information, please call or write:
Special Markets Department, HarperCollins Publishers,
10 East 53rd Street, New York, N.Y. 10022.
Telephone: (212) 207-7528. Fax: (212) 207-7222.

DUNCAN LONG

Night STALKERS

AVENGING STORM

HarperPaperbacks
A Division of HarperCollins*Publishers*

If you purchased this book without a cover, you should be
aware that this book is stolen property. It was reported as
"unsold and destroyed" to the publisher and neither the
author nor the publisher has received any payment for this
"stripped book."

This is a work of fiction. The characters, incidents, and
dialogues are products of the author's imagination and are not
to be construed as real. Any resemblance to actual events or
persons, living or dead, is entirely coincidental.

HarperPaperbacks   *A Division of* HarperCollins*Publishers*
                   10 East 53rd Street, New York, N.Y. 10022

Copyright © 1992 by Duncan Long
All rights reserved. No part of this book may be used or
reproduced in any manner whatsoever without written
permission of the publisher, except in the case of brief
quotations embodied in critical articles and reviews. For
information address HarperCollins*Publishers*,
10 East 53rd Street, New York, N.Y. 10022.

Cover illustration by Danilo Ducak

First printing: June 1992

Printed in the United States of America

HarperPaperbacks and colophon are trademarks of
HarperCollins*Publishers*

❖ 10 9 8 7 6 5 4 3 2 1

PROLOGUE

Tom and Kathy Baker trudged along the pink beach, damp sand under their bare feet. The Pacific sun bore down on them, hinting at the heat that would engulf the island when midday arrived. A wave, still cold from the previous night, crashed onto the shore, washing over the couple's feet and erasing their footprints.

"That bend in the cove is farther away than it looks," Tom remarked, pointing toward their goal up ahead. He studied the junglelike growth lining the beach. "I wish I'd brought my pistol," he added, half to himself.

"Oh, come on," Kathy laughed. "Islands don't have tigers or gorillas or anything, do they?"

"Well . . . No. Probably not," he conceded.

"We're the only dangerous things within a hundred miles of here," she chided. "You're Robinson Crusoe and I'm your girl Friday. Hey, let's see what's up there," she said, pointing toward the thick vegetation that ringed the beach. "I'd kill for some fresh fruit." She took his hand and tugged, walking along backward. "Come on."

"Okay," Tom replied, the reluctance in his voice suggesting he wasn't sure it was such a good idea.

"Race you to the tallest palm," Kathy challenged, breaking into a run before he could reply.

Tom hastily followed, pursuing a winding trail that ascended the brush-covered slope. He scrutinized the crumbling bank that jutted toward the beach and wondered what kind of snakes might be on the island.

Within two minutes they had topped the tiny hill at the base of the cliff, where Kathy came to a halt. "Look," she said breathlessly, pointing upward toward the towering palm overhead. "There *are* coconuts. Can you climb up to get them?"

Tom eyed the tall tree, rubbing his hand over its rough trunk, which bristled with sharp edges where leaf stems had once been. "I don't want to shinny up *this* thing," he protested. "I'd leave half my hide on the trunk. Besides," he added, shading his eyes as he looked upward, "I think the coconuts are all green."

"Let's follow this path on up the hill," she suggested, starting up the trail. "Maybe we can find some berries—"

"Wait just a minute," he cautioned. "I wonder if some kind of animal made this path? Look at these."

Kathy turned, glancing over her shoulder, then came to a stop. "What's wrong?"

"Look."

"If you're trying to play a trick on me—"

"I'm not," he protested. "We're not alone here at all."

As she neared the spot where he stood, she

spied what had attracted his attention. Footprints. "Ah, Robinson Crusoe has discovered the natives." She smiled.

Seeing his frown she added, "But we circled the island yesterday and didn't see any sign of anyone else."

"Yeah," he said, peering up and down the beach. "But I don't think we should hang around if . . ." His voice trailed off.

"Oh, come on. It's probably just—"

"No," he said, studying the trail as it advanced up the hill. "There're a bunch more tracks over there. Maybe eight or even ten people, from the looks of it."

"Or two that walked up and down the slope five times," she countered. "Besides, you said it looked like it hadn't rained for a while. These tracks could have been here a long time. Maybe someone stopped, looked around, and left long before we got here."

"Come on," Tom said, walking back down the path toward the beach. He could barely see their yawl through the foliage along the trail. The boat, anchored just a hundred yards offshore, bobbed up and down on the blue waves, laced with sunlight so bright it hurt his eyes. He turned back to Kathy. "Something doesn't feel right," he confided. "I think we should head back to the boat."

"Tom! Up on the ridge."

He turned. Looking toward where she pointed, he saw a group of men in tattered uniforms carrying rifles. Soldiers. They seemed to materialize out of the brush as he stared at them.

Tom swore under his breath. "Let's get the hell back to the boat!" he muttered. Clenching Kathy's hand, he half dragged her down the sandy incline in a panicky race toward the sea.

"What are they doing here—" Kathy gasped as they plunged pell-mell down the trail.

"Don't talk now," Tom gasped, nearly stumbling over a tree root that jutted across the sandy trail.

Something passed by Tom's head with a crack and thudded into the brush beside him. The report of a rifle echoed on the silent beach. *They're firing at us,* he thought with disbelief. Kathy whimpered and then was silent, gripping his hand so tightly it hurt as they continued to run.

With what seemed like agonizing slowness, they reached the beach; Tom steeled himself for another volley of fire, for the strike of a bullet he knew must come when the soldiers reached the beach, where they would have a clear shot at the couple.

Everything seemed deathly quiet. All he could hear was his breath and the crunching of the sand under his feet. *We're almost to the water,* he told himself, aware of the roar of the waves and realizing that the seagulls that had been scolding each other earlier had now vanished.

A voice called from behind him in what sounded like Japanese as he splashed into the water. "Hurry!" he yelled at Kathy, helping her keep her balance as they thrashed through the waves.

The bullet reached him before he heard the shot, slapping at his shoulder and stinging like a hornet's barb. His breath caught in his throat as he stumbled, falling to his knees in the water.

"Tom!" Kathy yelled, turning toward him.

"Go on! I'll catch up. Get to the boat."

"You're hurt."

"Don't come back!" he ordered, turning to see the soldiers that were now on the beach. "Get onto the boat."

Kathy hesitated and then waded back to him, supporting him as he struggled to his feet, half fighting her off. He turned to check on the soldiers' progress and was horrified to see them splashing into the ocean. One man, out ahead of the others, carried a long, curved sword in his hand.

Tom's mind raced as he and Kathy thrashed toward the boat. Why would soldiers be on the island, and why would they be dressed in such tattered uniforms. And a *sword*? he thought; it would be almost funny if it weren't so terrifying.

He could hear the splashing of the soldiers behind them and turned to appraise their progress. With horror, he saw the leader of the soldiers right behind him, sword flashing in the sunlight.

And then Tom lost consciousness, his head severed from his shoulders.

1

The wipers on the windscreen of the MH-60K SOA helicopter swish-sloshed back and forth, frantically sweeping the Plexiglas clear of the fat droplets that cascaded from the black sky. How quickly a training mission can be transformed into the real thing, Captain Jefferson Davis "Oz" Carson reflected, straining at the control column of the aircraft to keep it on its course above the churning ocean.

As a member of the U.S. Army's Night Stalkers helicopter team, which was part of Task Force 160 created from elements of the 158th Aviation Battalion and based in Fort Bragg, North Carolina, Oz normally engaged in special operations and antiterrorist work, although rescue missions were nothing new to him. A few hours after leaving their joint maneuvers with the Philippine army, the pilot and his crew had received word that they were to join U.S. Navy ships based offshore for a search and possible sea rescue effort.

But they seldom flew rescue missions at sea. And Oz hated being so far out over the ocean, where "setting down" meant abandoning a helicopter to a watery grave. *Give me solid ground any day,* the flier thought, examining the vertical situation display screen in front of him to check their flight path, horizon, and radar altitude. Satisfied he was still on their assigned search grid, he scanned the horizontal situation display, which provided flight projections, navigation reference points, and other pertinent information.

The pilot's eyes returned to the sea. Lightning silently danced across the clouds, making the water appear brighter than day behind the AN/PVS-6 night vision goggles he wore. Behind the helmet-mounted goggles, his blue eyes scanned the horizon, looking for some sign of the men who were lost and perhaps injured or dead.

"I think I see something," Lieutenant Harvey "O.T." Litwin's voice crackled over the intercom, accompanied by a peal of thunder that rattled the helicopter. The warrant officer rode in the gunner's cabin between the cockpit and the passenger compartment; "O.T." was short for "Old-Timer," since Litwin was the oldest crewman on the MH-60K. "Off port at about nine o'clock," he said. "The lightning reflected off something."

"I'm bringing us around," Oz said, kicking a rudder pedal and easing back on the control column to reduce their speed. "Luger, it'll come up on your side."

"I saw something light colored—within a hundred yards of us," O.T. told the specialist, who rode across from him in the gunner's compartment.

"Okay, I'll keep my eyes peeled," SP4 Mike Luger responded over the intercom. In contrast to

O.T., Luger was the youngest man aboard—and looked even younger than his twenty years, thanks to a fair complexion and the thin, muscled body of a jogger.

The pilot completed his turn and kicked the right rudder pedal to straighten out their course. He glanced toward his navigator. "Death Song, you see anything in the FLIR?"

"Negative on the FLIR," the Native American reported, carefully studying the view screen on the forward-looking infrared scope that was capable of spotting men in the water by their heat signature.

Oz checked the horizontal situation display screen to be sure he was on course and then shook his head. Their assignment had been simple enough: locate and pick up an oil drilling crew from the sea. But even finding any trace of the wreckage—let alone the crew—was another matter; the Australian ship, an experimental drilling vessel searching for oil, had failed to radio its position just as surely as it had failed to release its mooring lines in time. The ship was capsized by the winds coming in ahead of the growing typhoon.

A gust battered the MH-60K, whipping them sideward over the lurching sea below. *Have we finally found something, or is this just another bit of flotsam?* Oz wondered. A lot of junk floated on the surface of the ocean, creating continual false sightings.

The black mantle of clouds hinted at the fury of the typhoon, now designated "Norman," that would soon reach the area the helicopter patrolled. They were nearing the end of their patrol, and the pilot debated with himself whether to refuel and return or scrub the mission until after the storm had passed. Scrubbing would be safest for the Night Stalkers—and would likely be a death sentence for any survivors from the drilling ship. It would be a very hard choice, and Oz knew it would probably fall to him to make for himself and his men. It was a choice he didn't care to think about for the time being.

He studied the rolling waves on the ocean's surface, which the wind kicked higher and higher as the typhoon approached. "See anything, Luger?"

"Not a thing," the gunner answered. "Hang on . . . Yes! Directly to starboard about two hundred feet."

"I see it, too," Death Song said, glancing out his right window. "At three o'clock."

Oz kicked the helicopter around, taking them closer to the position indicated.

Death Song glanced at the view screen in front of him. "There's no FLIR signature. Whatever it is, it's the same temp as the water."

"It's a life jacket," Luger announced.

"Yeah," Death Song agreed. "And there's some plastic bottles of some kind off to the right of us."

Oz eased the control column forward, sending the helicopter forward. "There's no doubt we must be close to where they went down. I see some more wreckage straight ahead."

"Whole lot more off port," O.T. added.

"This has to be it." Oz inched them toward port and shoved the control column forward to take them toward the debris that bobbed on the quaking surface of the ocean. He scrutinized the sea as they advanced, his night vision goggles transforming the swirling water into varying shades of green and white that were brightly lit from time to time by lightning flashes. He tensed the stiff muscles in his long legs, fighting the gale that pushed them off course.

"I'm picking up an intermittent signal on the emergency frequency!" Death Song exclaimed.

"Emergency beacon?" Oz asked the navigator.

"Yeah. Looks like just one. Very, very faint."

"There're a couple of flashlights coming on, too," O.T.'s voice said from the back. "Whoever's down there is trying to signal us."

"Death Song, bring up the coordinates on the VSD," Oz ordered, bringing the control column to its center position and slowing the MH-60K; he lowered the collective pitch lever, dropping them closer to the water as he neared the flashing lights below.

Men in life jackets bobbed among the debris, waving frantically to the helicopter.

The pilot pulled the control column into its center position, bringing the helicopter to a hover above the Australian sailors. He toggled his radio on. "CV-63, this is NS-1. Come in please."

The radio crackled in his headphones. "NS-1, this is CV-63. We read you."

"CV-63, we've found survivors. Repeat, we have confirmed sighting of survivors. We have an emergency beacon signal at"—the pilot glanced at the coordinates Death Song had punched onto the vertical situation display screen—"ninety-five degrees due north, our map coordinates AAB, 872.

We're in position now, homing in an emergency beacon with flashlight signals from the surface. Looks like there's a bunch of men in the water."

"Good work, NS-1. We'll relay your message to the other choppers so they can converge on your position. Over."

"Any word on the weather?"

"NS-1, we were about to call you. We've received an advisory from the U.S. Weather Bureau that the worst of the storm is headed our way. You need to get back ASAP. Over."

"We read you," Oz replied. "How much time do we have?"

"They're estimating Norman will peak at 220 kph in about a half hour."

Oz whistled. "Okay. We'll work fast. In the meantime we could use some assistance. Can any of the other copter's get here in time to help?"

"We'll have two more in position shortly. ETA five minutes. The commander is going to pull the rest back to the ship and will be grounding them so we can get them stowed before Norman hits."

"Have your deck crew and medics on standby when we come in," Oz ordered. "We're going to be racing the storm when we come. Over."

"That's a big roger, NS-1. Good luck."

"Thanks. Over and out." The pilot switched to the intercom. "Gentlemen, time to get to work."

2

Major Yoshiro Tashida settled onto the crudely woven cushion, cradling his *katana* in his hands for a moment, remembering the ceremony during which he had received the magnificent sword. The war with the Americans had just started, and he had been recalled to duty for his Emperor, Hirohito.

"My military-issue sword will serve me well," Tashida had gently explained to his father as the two stood in the old man's room.

"Yes, but not as well as this sword." His father held his treasured *katana* out to the young man.

Tashida hesitated. To touch the scabbard of a samurai sword was forbidden.

"Do not be afraid to hold it," his father said, presenting the blade to the young man's trembling hands. "For it belongs to you."

Tashida's eyes blurred with tears as he took the ancient *katana*, hand forged by the master swordsmith Muramasa in the fourteenth century. "I will never bring dishonor to this sword," the young man vowed.

"That is why you must have it."

Now Tashida was as old and gray as his father had been, the gnarled hands that removed the blade from its scabbard lined like those of his father. *What has happened to my father and family?* he wondered, carefully holding the blade to avoid touching the steel with his fingers.

He and his men had religiously guarded the island half a century for the emperor; during that time many small boats had been captured, and the oil on the cloth with which he wiped the blade of his sword had come from one of those vessels. Tashida had become not only the military leader but the leader of what had become a *dôzoku*, an extended family encompassing his men and their families.

But the invasion of the island, for which they had all prepared, never came; instead, the great war with America, Britain, and Australia apparently continued, dragging on now for decades, like a long anticlimax to an ill-conceived *No* play.

The major used broad strokes over the *mimigata*, temper lines along the edge of the blade, and then paused to rub the tiny *kizu,* a pencil-dot imperfection in the otherwise perfect blade, with the oiled rag. For a moment Tashida saw his face reflected in the blade and smiled at himself, proud of the work he'd done in holding the island for the emperor.

Of course there had been precious little fighting since 1945, when the activities of both the enemy and the Japanese had seemingly ground to a near standstill. Since his radio had been damaged beyond repair in the winter of 1944, Tashida and his men had continued guarding the out-of-the-way member of the South Pacific's Solomon Islands, little by little upgrading the fortifications on the island, honeycombing it into an underground city.

In fact the soldiers in his *dôzoku* had become almost self-sufficient, now producing their own crude cloth and scavenging enough equipment from the few boats they captured to keep their tanks and weapons in repair. Recently his men had even perfected the process of refining vegetable oils for the lamps they used to light the underground passageways and rooms.

As was the practice of Japanese officers, when they had left their country, five of his officers had brought their wives and children with them to the island. Most of his other men had long since taken wives from the native population who had originally occupied the island when Tashida had taken it over.

The soldiers' sons now helped to perpetuate the modern-day samurai society Major Tashida had created. With the native population and the few outsiders they'd captured acting as slaves, the Japanese-held island had remained under the empire's control, with only an occasional private yacht straying into the area to be captured and cannibalized for parts.

Tashida pulled out the bamboo peg securing the hilt to the sword blade and removed the silk-and-ray handle from the tang. He paused to study the characters on the tang, which attested to the prowess of the blade that had been tested by the master swordsmith on prisoners; the marks certified that it had cut two men in half with one stroke. Tashida rubbed oil onto the tang and its markings; since that first test of the blade, it had continued to draw more than its share of enemy blood in the hands of Tashida's family. He carefully replaced the hilt on the razor-sharp curved blade.

After returning the sword to its sheath and setting both on their ceremonial stand or *katanakake,* he rose, picked up his oil lantern, and left the tiny room.

"Major," his first officer, Lieutenant Noboru Ishimoto, said as Tashida entered the adjoining room, dimly lit and smelling of damp earth and burned oil.

The major set his lantern on the crude wooden table, and the yellow light glowed off the dirt and bamboo walls. "What news do you have?"

"We have the radio from aboard the boat we captured today."

"Is it like the others?" Tashida asked.

"Even smaller and in perfect working order," Ishimoto answered. "Yet we receive nothing on our frequency but odd American music. Is it possible our army has forgotten about us?"

"No, they have not forgotten us," Tashida answered, looking directly at the old officer and studying his narrow, lined face for a moment. "That is only what the Americans want us to think, to destroy our morale after all these years. The ability of the Americans to create such tiny equipment puzzles me. Doubly so since so much of it is labeled with the English characters representing

Japan. Is this equipment so?"

"Yes, Major. How do they manage to become so advanced, and why do they engage in such elaborate schemes?"

Tashida said nothing. In fact, when the channels other than the one reserved for coded signals from the emperor's generals to their troops were listened to, it sounded as if there was no war going on at all. The major had no good explanation for why the Allies had gone to such elaborate lengths to make it seem that there was no war. They had even created an imaginary world where many countries—including Japan—cooperated with one another.

"The main thing is that we know the schemes are false," Tashida finally said. "We know they cannot be true. The Americans have never understood *Nippon* and have failed to understand the samurai code of *Bushido*." Both men knew that to surrender is forbidden to true warriors; Japan would either triumph or commit mass *seppuku*. For the samurai race, there was no middle ground, no surrender. For the emperor, who had descended from the sun itself, to surrender was unthinkable; the people of Japan would destroy their country and themselves before such a thing occurred.

"But why this elaborate scheme?" Ishimoto asked.

Tashida had asked himself the same question a thousand times. He shook his head to tell his officer, "I have no answer." And why didn't their army contact them on the code frequency? the major wondered. Of course that was easily explained: the frequencies on the dial could have been altered. Without their original radio, it was impossible to determine what the frequencies really were.

Finally Tashida spoke. "The Americans are treacherous. That is what we must keep in mind. I have to wonder how many of our people have given themselves up and been slaughtered because of these elaborate broadcasts. The Americans are a devious, mongrel race. Put the radio with the others; we don't want our men to be misled by the broadcasts."

"*Hai*," Ishimoto answered, bowing before he turned to leave, but his face betrayed the fact that something else was on his mind.

"What else?" the major asked.

"The woman you captured today?"

Tashida's face clouded over. The woman had undoubtedly been sent to spy on the island. While she couldn't hurt them now, she would have to die; the major didn't want to risk the diluting of their race—the native wives his men had taken were bad enough. *Nippon* traced its lineage back to the sun goddess herself, unlike the other inferior races with their light pink or dark black skins—inferiors in mind and body. "Strip her and give her to the young men to do with as they want. Just be sure she's dead by morning."

"*Hai*." Ishimoto bowed again, turned, and left.

One thing is sure, the major told himself, settling down on the mat in front of the low table: the American's treachery had got them nowhere on his island. He and his men still held Kakira, and it would be impossible for anyone to root them out of the fortress without severe losses. Like the other islands and lands in the Empire of the Sun, Kakira would be held as long as a single Japanese soldier remained alive on it.

Let the Americans come so he could do with them as he had done to the woman spy they had sent to his island.

3

Luger held onto the door frame of the helicopter, eyeing the heaving water below. The gale hammered furiously at the MH-60K, tearing at the machine and making their hover impossible for the pilot to maintain. The drenched gunner stood at the open side door of the chopper.

"Want me to go down?" O.T. asked Oz over the intercom. "We've got the winch set to go."

"Negative on that," Oz replied. "Let's let Luger take it this time. He's about eighty pounds lighter than you are, and if a bunch of those guys panic and try to grab on, we're that much less apt to snap our line."

"Yes, sir," O.T. replied, giving the other gunner a thumbs-up sign. "And that's a mighty tricky way to suggest I go on a diet, sir."

Luger chuckled but said nothing as he snapped the STABO harness around himself and latched it into the end of the wire cable dangling outside the door. He tugged it to be sure it was tight and then jerked the release on his life vest so the gas canister in it puffed it up with a loud hiss.

"Better take off the helmet," O.T. said over the intercom.

Luger nodded with a grin and raised his night vision goggles. He unsnapped the chin strap and removed his helmet, setting it down where it couldn't roll out. Turning back toward the doorway, he was abruptly aware of the darkness beyond the red emergency lights of the cabin. He looked at O.T. "Sure is dark," he yelled.

"Don't worry," O.T. yelled back. "Oz's turning on the landing lights now. You'll do great."

"Tell the captain I'm ready."

O.T. spoke into the intercom, then turned back to Luger. "The captain says it's going to be pretty tough going with the wind and waves."

"Just bring me back up each time and I won't complain," the young gunner replied. Swallowing nervously, he again tugged at the SH-60B-style rescue hoist mounted over the door frame to assure himself it really could hold him and then, without pausing for fear of losing his confidence, he inched toward the doorway and carefully lowered himself over the side so only the thin steel cord supported his weight.

Swinging back and forth as he descended, Luger looked upward at the helicopter that seemed to rise above him, its bright landing lights sending a cone of light downward. He glanced toward his feet to see the water rising to meet him as the thin steel cable spooled out of the winch. Within seconds his boots touched the water, which felt warm compared to the cool air around him. He sank into the murky liquid as it swelled upward, buoying him on his flotation vest.

"Over here," a voice cried from the darkness.

Luger thrashed in the water, turning toward a seaman who seemed deathly pale in the bright light coming from the helicopter. The gunner choked as a wave rose over his head, creating near panic before he bobbed back to the surface; he swore, spitting the foul-tasting brine, and then half swam, half floated toward the sailor who was swimming toward him.

"Man," the sailor yelled, his voice quivering from the cold, "I didn't think you guys'd *ever* get here."

"Grab on," Luger shouted back. "Hold tight. Don't have time to fasten you into a harness."

"Just get me out of here."

"Get your legs wrapped around my waist and hang on. Don't choke me!"

"Sorry, mate."

Luger struggled to get an arm free as he glanced up at the helicopter hovering above, its bright landing light and the spray created by the wake of the chopper's blades causing him to squint. Trying to blink his eyes clear, he gave the ready-for-pickup signal by holding his right hand in the air, palm forward.

The winch was activated, and the steel cable reeled the pair in like human fish; after gyrating wildly in the wind, the two were finally alongside the chopper's open door.

Luger reached out and grabbed O.T.'s hand, and the warrant officer rocked the men outward and then hauled them back onto the edge of the doorway. "Get over there," O.T. directed the sailor after throwing a Mylar emergency blanket around him. The warrant officer leaned toward Luger and hollered over the noise of the helicopter: "Looks like there are at least ten more down there."

"Piece of cake." Luger grinned, teeth chattering. He stepped back toward the open doorway. "At least I can't get any wetter."

O.T. nodded, then activated the winch and lowered the young gunner back toward the heaving water below.

"We see your strobes," Oz radioed to the other helicopter approaching them. "Don't get in too close or we'll need someone to fish us out of the drink."

"That's a roger, NS-1," the pilot of the other chopper answered. "This wind is getting impossible to deal with. We've got all the sailors out of the water over here, so this is as close as we'll get for the time being. Over."

"Good. When you have the last one aboard, you'd better head back. We're about finished here, and with the five you have and the nine over here, it sounds like the whole crew is accounted for, from what the sailors we have aboard say. Over."

"We'll be heading back then—our guy is on the cable now. Don't stay out too long, NS-1."

"Roger that. I'll talk to you later. Over and out." Oz toggled off the radio and switched to the intercom. "How's it going, O.T.?"

"Luger's headed down for the last one now. Hang on. Look's like he's having some trouble. Our cable is . . . Hang on."

Abruptly the helicopter sagged toward the water. Oz compensated with the collective pitch lever, easing it downward for fear of injuring the gunner on the end of the steel cable hanging from the side of the helicopter. The pilot knew what had happened before O.T.'s voice crackled over the earphones: "Luger's got snagged in the debris. Doesn't look like he can get himself free."

Luger cursed, fighting to get his head above the water. He hadn't seen the long plastic conduit that had been floating nearly hidden in the water, as he had dropped back down to pick up the last sailor near the Night Stalkers' helicopter. When he had spotted the debris he'd tried to avoid dropping onto it, but his efforts had only succeeded in looping the steel cable around the huge pipe, which spun away from him as he tried to grab its slick surface. The cable twisted as the conduit rolled, dragging him below its surface.

Now, for a moment, a wave buoyed him upward and he was able to get his head above water. He sputtered and took a deep breath of air as the wave passed and the line tightened, dragging him back under the plastic pipe. *Got to get free of the line*, he thought. But the cable held his chest tight against the conduit, and he was unable to reach the release of the STABO harness.

His lungs nearly breaking, he waited an eternity for the next wave to come. The sea rose and the line loosened. His fingers grappled with the latch and then he was free. He kicked clear of the cable and pipe, slowly floating upward until his head again broke the surface and he gasped for air, coughing when the spray soaked into his nose and open mouth.

"Hang on, partner," an unfamiliar voice with a thick Australian accent called to the airman.

Pushing the water from his eyes, Luger blinked and turned to see one of the sailors swimming next to him, his damp hair sparkling in the landing lights of the chopper above.

"Thought you were a goner," the sailor said. "Tried to get over here to help you but couldn't make it any sooner—broke my ankle when our ship capsized."

"I'm okay now," Luger answered. "But if they can't get that cable free, we're all in deep shit."

"So what else is new?"

"The cable won't come free," O.T. yelled over the intercom. "It's tight—about to break from the look of it—and whatever it's caught on is barely rising out of the water."

Oz thought a moment. If the cable broke, there was a good chance that it would fly down and hit Luger or the sailor in the water. Or it might spring upward into the helicopter's rotors. While neither was even probable, the outside possibility of such a disaster made chancing it too risky. There was only one thing to do. "Use the emergency release."

"But how will we get Luger if—"

"Just do it."

Samuel Edmonton, the captain of the American cruise ship *Pleasure Run,* watched the rain that pelted the front port of the bridge, reducing visibility to zero. He was distracted by the abrupt sound of wind and the splatter of rain when the port hatch was unbolted and a crewman came in, soaked to the bone.

Edmonton waited for the sailor to secure the hatchway behind himself; this job completed, the underling turned toward the captain, who stood by the helmsman.

"Everything's secured, Captain," the sailor reported.

"How are our passengers?"

"The doc's dispensing Dramamine as fast as he can make his way around the rooms. He said to tell you that his nurse is sick in her cabin as well."

Captain Edmonton said nothing. The nurse had been a bone of contention between him and the doctor all along, and the captain had finally hired her when there was no other qualified applicant for the position before they sailed.

"Just let me do it alone," Doc had said, his elu-

27

sive smile flickering across his face for a moment and vanishing as if it had never been there. "Why waste the money?"

But Edmonton had hired her anyway, and now she was sick in her bunk. "That will be all then," he told the crewman. "Better get back to your quarters and get into some dry clothes."

"Aye, sir."

The captain turned back to the helmsman and then glanced at the radar. Everything looked all right. He grasped the long brass railing ahead of the helm as the tour ship mounted a towering wave and plummeted back down the watery slope. Normally rough seas weren't that bad in a ship the size of the *Pleasure Run*.

"Quite a storm blowing up," the helmsman said, as if reading the captain's thoughts.

"That it is," the captain replied. "What are we getting from the weather bureau?" he asked his radioman.

"Still sounds like we're going to be nearly in the center of the typhoon, Captain."

Edmonton glanced back out the front port and then paced across the wide steel bridge, leaning to keep his balance as the 250-foot ship lurched and another lightning flash illuminated the ocean. Built in 1958, the *Pleasure Run* had weathered more than its fair share of storms. Normally the cruise ship traveled the calmer waters of the Mediterranean; the idea of a round-the-world cruise had appealed to him when he'd started. But now he was sick of it and ready to be home.

"Uh, Captain, do you think we should radio our

position?" the radioman asked, turning away from his console.

"No," Edmonton snapped, his tone telling the crewman that he didn't care to discuss the situation further. The captain knew he could be in a real mess, if they ran into any trouble, since it was likely that the authorities would come aboard and nose around; they'd done it before, when INTERPOL thought—but had never been able to prove—that the *Pleasure Run* was involved in smuggling. With all the drugs being smuggled these days, government agents of all kinds made it their business to snoop whenever possible.

Edmonton had never knowingly allowed drugs to be smuggled on board any ship he captained. But he couldn't afford having his ship searched since, in addition to the 520 crew members and passengers aboard, he'd taken on an illegal cargo of firearms, shoulder-launched missiles, and small arms ammunition from China; stowed in the forward hold, they would be spotted easily by anyone carefully inspecting the ship.

He couldn't afford to radio for help or even give their position for fear of attracting attention. Instead he'd ordered his crew and passengers to batten down and hoped to weather the storm.

Hell, he thought, *as big and sudden as this storm is, we'd have had to batten down and be on our own anyway*. Unless they went down, contacting the authorities wouldn't have done them any good—and might have caused someone to come snoop around afterward. No, he'd done the right thing in not radioing their position. "Keep a close watch on the radar," he told the crewman sitting in front of the console. "You're our eyes tonight, and it's possible someone may be way off course."

"Right, Captain," the technician replied, studying the scope with renewed interest under the captain's watchful eye as the ship reeled upward on another swell.

The intercom phone rang. "I'll take that," Edmonton said, crossing toward the bulkhead and lifting the headset. "This is the captain."

"Captain," the voice on the other side hollered. "Engineering. We're having some more trouble with our forward boiler. Looks like it's going to have to be shut down so we can check its gauges."

"What!" Edmonton yelled, causing all the crewmen in the bridge to turn toward him and then quickly turn back to their tasks as he glared at them. The captain lowered his voice as he spoke again. "Look, I need full power up here so we can head into this storm. If we lose power we'll get blown halfway across the Pacific to who knows where. Keep that thing going. That's an order."

"We'll try, Captain, but—"

Edmonton slammed the phone back onto its cradle and paced back to the view port stretching across the forward wall of the bridge. Damn it all, he thought. If things weren't bad enough, the boilers were acting up again. Not that they didn't have to be babied like everything else on the decrepit tub.

The captain made a solemn vow that if he ever got through the ordeal facing him this night, his smuggling days were over.

* * *

Mike Johnson, the engineer of the *Pleasure Run,* hung up the intercom phone, his black face an angry mask. The captain was often hard to work with, but this took the cake. However it was probably to be expected.

The captain's acted like he's had a bee up his butt for the entire cruise, the Afro-American thought.

The engineer could understand the captain's situation, however. If the engines lost full power in this storm, there'd be hell to pay. He turned to the sailor at the brightly lit control center that monitored the engines powering the twin screws of the ship. "Be ready to cut power to half if our forward boiler has to be shut down," he ordered. "We don't want to damage our engines."

"Yes, sir," the seaman answered, his hand unconsciously edging toward the controls.

The humming of the turbines changed almost imperceptibly, but Johnson noted the ominous pitch. He crossed to the side of the U-shaped control console and checked the power of the turbines: it was nowhere near optimum. That didn't make sense, because the gauges for the forward boiler showed it was going full tilt and should be giving them more than enough power. He'd had men checking for steam leaks but there were none. Nothing suggested what was wrong, yet something was certainly inaccurate or malfunctioning.

He turned to the sailor in front of the boiler gauges. "What have you got with the boiler?"

"Our gauges on the forward boiler are in the red and continuing up," the crewman announced.

Johnson double-checked the gauges over

the man's shoulder.

"Still climbing, sir," the sailor warned.

"I can see that," Johnson whispered. The needles were well in the red, almost halfway through the "danger" printed at the far reading of the dials; he'd ordered the men at the console to shut off the warning alarms fifteen minutes ago. Surely the problem was with the sensors or gauges, since the boiler was barely putting out enough power to keep the turbine engines running at full-ahead power.

But on the other hand, Johnson had never seen all the sensors or gauges on a console malfunction at once; usually they failed one at a time. If the pressure really was building up to that level, something would give, and more than likely the boiler itself would rupture or even explode.

The needles proceeded upward little by little as he watched.

Johnson rubbed his bald spot and then gave his order. "Let's take it to half speed."

"Engines to half speed," the crewman at the board called, jacking the controls into position.

"Turn off the line to the forward boiler burners," the engineer directed the other sailor.

"Forward burners shutting down."

"Open the emergency release valves."

"Emergency valves released."

Johnson grimaced as the steam rattled through the pipes ahead of the engine room and then he stepped across to the intercom phone and picked it up. The deck lurched as the storm pounded the ship, already shoving it off course as the screws wound down to half speed.

5

"Crack open the cargo access hatch and lower something through it," Oz instructed O.T. over the intercom. "We have any other cable?"

"No," O.T. said grimly, struggling to unscrew the lugs holding the hatch in place on the floor. The bolts were slick with brine, and his fingers grew stiff from the chill wind blowing into the helicopter. The hatch was designed to give emergency access to the cargo hook below the chopper should the pilot be unable to release the load from the cockpit.

Finally O.T. had the last lug off and pulled the hatch away, exposing a large square opening that showed the heaving sea below them. "Got it open," the warrant officer said, holding on to the back of a seat to keep from falling through the opening as the helicopter rocked violently in the wind.

"Do the guys back there have belts on?" Oz asked over the intercom.

"Good idea," O.T. replied, crossing to the passenger compartment. "Listen up," he shouted to the sailors around him. "Our cable's busted and we don't have any way to get the last two guys back up to the chopper. Let's see if we can make a rope out of our belts. What's everybody got on?"

O.T. watched in the red-lit cabin as the men stood and quickly removed the belts from the uniforms they wore. All but one of the belts were heavy nylon with thick locking clasps, perfect for the task at hand. Rapidly the warrant officer connected the belts together, placing the end of one into the buckle of the next, testing them as he worked to be sure they would hold.

Wish I had some time to tape those buckles, he thought when he'd finished. If one of the buckles got caught on something it could pop open and the whole thing would come loose. But there wasn't time to find a way to secure them, he decided. It would have to do.

The warrant officer eyed the length that he had and made a quick mental calculation before calling on the intercom. "It's going to be close. Looks like we have about twenty-six feet of belts. Is that enough?"

"The waves are getting pretty high," Oz replied. "But I guess twenty-six feet is going to have to be enough, isn't it?"

"Yes, sir. Hang on a minute while I secure our makeshift line to something back here."

"Do you have enough manpower to haul them up?"

"Yeah," the warrant officer answered, unlatching the belt on the end of the series. "I think there're enough of us to pull them up." He quickly looped the belt around the pole supporting the wall between the gunner's and passenger compartments, then put its end back through the buckle of the next belt and refastened it to the others. Satisfied the belts were secured to the pole, he squatted down and tossed the free end through the open hatch in the floor. "Okay," he said into his helmet mike. "I think we're as ready as we're going to get to pick them up."

"Guide us in, then," Oz ordered his warrant officer.

O.T. knelt at the edge of the open hatch and searched for Luger and the sailor bobbing in the water below. He could barely see the heads of the two men bouncing in the waves. "Forward about five yards."

"Heave," a burly sailor shouted over the thunderous beating of the helicopter rotors and the storm outside. With this command the four sailors leaning through the open hatchway lifted upward while their compatriots gathered round to lift the slack line.

"Watch you don't hit the buckles," O.T. cautioned.

"Right, we don't want to drop him back into the brine," one of the sailors agreed.

"Ready," the first sailor warned. "Heave!"

The men repeated the process over and over, laboring to bring the sailor up the line until he was finally a foot from the hatchway. Then those not holding the line of belts reached down over the backs of their comrades and grabbed the sailor's life vest as he dangled beneath the chopper. With cries and groans, they dragged the sailor upward through the hatchway.

"Bloody hell," the sailor cried as he tumbled onto the wet floor. "If you guys aren't a sight for sore eyes."

O.T. rapidly untied the fat knot around the sailor's waist. "Stand back," he ordered the men around the hatch and, as they stepped back, he tossed the line downward toward the rolling waves.

"Damn. Visibility is almost zero," one of the sailors cried. "I don't see your buddy down there anymore."

"We've lost sight of Luger," O.T. called on the intercom. "I can't see him anywhere."

"I have him on the FLIR," Death Song replied. "He's about ten meters ahead of us. But I can't see the belts to guide them to him."

"We need to get the line right to him," O.T. said. "With that wind flapping it around, a man in the water can't swim quickly enough to grab it."

"Can you fasten something hot to the end of the cable?" Oz asked. "Like a flare, maybe?"

"Good idea," O.T. said. He rapidly pulled the belts back up and jerked a flare and some duct tape out of the storage compartment next to him. He yanked a length of tape off the reel, then ripped it with his teeth and secured the flare to the end of a belt. "Stand back," he warned the sailors as he stepped toward the open floor hatch. He tugged the cord on the flare and it sputtered to life, lighting the dim interior of the cabin with its brilliant white flame. Gingerly the warrant officer dropped the glowing stick through the open hatch.

"I've got it on the FLIR," Death Song announced. "OK, forward ten feet and a little to the right," the navigator instructed Oz. "Forward a little more . . . There!"

O.T. squinted through the open hatch. "There he is!" he shouted. "He's taking the flare off the belts. It will take him a minute to get the belt tied around him."

The waves dropped out from under the helicopter as O.T. watched, leaving Luger hanging, holding onto the belts with one hand.

"Hang on," O.T. half whispered, willing the airman to keep his grasp on the swaying belts.

The waves rose again and the airman was buoyed by them. Luger looped the belts around his waist and gave the lift signal as the sea dropped out from under him.

"Haul him aboard," O.T. shouted, seeing the signal. The helicopter seemed to shiver as the wind caught it, then jerked back as Oz compensated for the motion.

"Heave!" the sailor cried, and the men lying next to the hatch reached down and lifted the line, holding it until their companions took up the slack, then repositioning themselves to repeat the process.

"Heave!" the sailor ordered again and the airman slowly ascended toward the helicopter. The waves lapped upward, throwing spray through the open hatchway.

One of the sailors shook the water from his eyes, letting the belts scrape against the edge of the metal hatchway.

"Watch the buckles!" O.T. yelled to the man. But his warning was too late.

One of the belts scraped across the edge of the hatchway, and the buckle unlatched, freeing the belt it held. The freed nylon rapidly snaked out of the buckle and dropped through the open hatchway.

The sailor closest to it clawed at the belt slipping past him, momentarily slowing it before it was torn from his grasp. But at the same instant O.T., who had thrown himself toward the vanishing belt, snatched it in both his meaty paws and clung to it as if his life depended on it, oblivious of the fact that he was dragged with it through the open hatchway.

As O.T. had hoped, the hands of those around him clamped onto his life belt and legs, holding and then lifting him back into the helicopter.

"Hang on!" the sailor closest to his ear cried.

O.T. said nothing. He clenched the belt and its buckle, the metal and nylon edges cutting into his hands. He ground his teeth, ignoring the pain and willing himself not to let go of the swaying line.

Hang on, hang on, hang on, he told himself over and over again as he was pulled back into the rocking helicopter.

Finally the sailors could reach the belt, and they took over. "You can let go now," one of them told O.T. "We'll have him aboard in a minute."

The warrant officer stepped back into the compartment and watched, his hands too cut and bloody to be of help. Within a minute Luger was aboard.

"Late as usual," O.T. chided the shivering airman as he threw an emergency blanket over his partner's shoulders.

Luger pulled the blanket around his thin frame. "I saw what you did, and I—"

"Better find a seat, everyone," O.T. interrupted, patting the gunner on the shoulder. "Get buckled in." The warrant officer shoved the plug from his helmet into an intercom outlet, wondering if the cord had been frayed by the frantic leap through the hatchway. "Captain? Can you hear me?"

"O.T., you've got my undivided attention. What's going on back there?"

"I'll tell you later, it's a little complicated. But we're all aboard and ready to head in."

"Great. Now hang on," Oz warned. "We've got some pretty rough sledding ahead of us if we're going to make it back before the worst of this hits."

6

Captain Edmonton slammed the intercom onto its cradle and swore under his breath. *Now we're in a real mess,* he fumed, sullenly watching the rain that pelted the front port of the bridge. The ship would soon be drifting out of control if he didn't bring it around.

Better get into action, he ordered himself. "Flood the port ballast tanks," he ordered.

"Flood port ballast tanks," the helmsman ordered, speaking into the intercom at his station.

The captain paced across the narrow bridge, hands clenched behind his back, as the ship rocked under his feet and gradually started to list to the port side as the tanks at the bottom of the hull filled with brine. *Hopefully the list will counter the wind as we turn,* Edmonton thought to himself. In theory the ship would list enough, though no one in his right mind ever made a turn in seas like this if it could possibly be avoided: the chance of capsizing was too great.

"Port ballast tanks are flooded, Captain."

Edmonton swallowed and forced himself not

to cross his fingers. "Pump out the starboard ballast tanks."

"Activate starboard ballast tank pumps."

The captain waited a few moments to be sure there were no problems with the pumps and then gave his order. "Left full rudder. One hundred eighty degrees."

The helmsman's face paled, even though he knew the command would be coming once the order to flood the tanks had been given. "Left full rudder," he repeated, bringing the wheel slowly around in shaky hands. "Commencing one-hundred-eighty-degree-turn."

The *Pleasure Run* slowly turned in the storm, its port side taking the pounding of the wind and waves. Despite the extra weight in the ballast tanks on the port side, the ship started to list to the right as the wind and waves caught its side. The crewmen on the bridge grabbed ahold of equipment or the brass rails running around the helm and outside walls, and the ship shook like a huge animal, its metal deck and walls vibrating as the sea pounded it.

The captain gritted his teeth as he watched the compass swing around. *The halfway point,* he thought. "Gentlemen, hold on to your hats," he said, trying to inject some levity into the mood of those around him. Instead his words fell flat. His eyes were on the compass as the ship continued to list at an ever steeper angle.

An unattended coffee mug slid noisily across the radar console and, despite the rimmed edge on the counter, tumbled off and shattered on the floor. Edmonton glanced around. "Leave it for later," he ordered the nervous sailor at the scope who started to get up. "Keep an eye out so we will be aware of anything that we're facing on our new course."

"Aye, Captain."

If we make it to the new course, Edmonton added to himself. The ship leaned over at an even steeper angle, and he wondered how long it would be before it rolled over onto its side. He watched the compass continue to swing around; they were past the halfway mark.

The ship started to right itself.

Got to act quickly, now, Edmonton told himself. "Flood the starboard ballast tanks."

"Flood starboard tanks."

The captain paced across the bridge again as the ship leveled out, the wind to its stern. *And to be driven to God only knows where.* "Gentlemen, I believe we made it. It was a little tense, but we made it."

"A *little* tense, Captain," the helmsman replied, wiping the sweat off his brow with the back of his hand.

Edmonton forced a smile as he studied the haggard faces around him. "Keep an eye on that radar," he ordered, his voice again possessing its forceful ring of authority. "We're out of the worst of it but we're going to have to stay sharp so we can avoid running into anything that the wind drives us at."

He looked through the forward port. "Turn on all our lights. I want us to look like a Christmas tree. You can't see far in this storm, but if there's any other ship ahead of us, I want them to see us coming from as far away as possible." Edmonton glanced at the compass and then turned toward his navigator. "Zellerman, let's get the maps out and see where we're headed."

"Aye, Captain."

Engineer Johnson inspected the massive steel access plate leading to the forward boiler. "If I could lay my hands on the clown that painted over these bolts I'd personally strangle him," the engineer said, selecting a wrench from his belt and placing its half-moon end around the bottom lug of the plate.

He strained at the bolt and finally it snapped loose. "At least the paint's not too old," he muttered. Slowly he removed each of the bolts until only one remained. "All right, get a tight hold on it," he ordered the two crewmen assisting him.

The men, Ken Cox and Dan Fernandez, grasped the rings on either side of the heavy steel plate, then leaned against the bulkhead of the swaying ship to keep their balance. "All right. We've got it," Cox told the engineer.

Johnson hoped they really did have a good grip. He'd seen more than a few toes broken during his four decades on the sea. He stepped back so his own feet would be clear of the edge of the plate if it fell, set his wrench over the last bolt, and threw his weight against it, torquing it counter-clockwise. The bolt screeched and then suddenly came free, causing Johnson to skin his knuckles on the side of the gasket.

No one said anything as he sucked his knuckles, holding the wrench as if he'd smack either of the crewmen if they made a wisecrack. Then he placed the tool back into position and twisted it again to overcome the tight threads until the bolt finally started turning freely. After six complete rotations, the bolt was nearly out of its hole. "Almost there," he warned his helpers. "Hang on."

As he continued a final twist, the bolt abruptly popped out of its hole. The heavy steel plate with its rubber gasket dropped three inches before the two sailors assisting him caught and supported it.

Johnson dropped the wrench to the steel deck, where it clanged noisily, then grabbed the edge of the cover. "Let's set it over there," he grunted, pointing with his chin. The three crab-walked carefully, since the ship now rolled and listed with each wave. When they reached the bulkhead, they gently set the plate down on its back.

"That should take about ten years off our spines," Johnson said, straightening stiffly. "Cox, get the flashlights over here so we can see what's going on in the boiler."

"Yes, sir." The sailor quickly collected three heavy flashlights and brought them over to Johnson and Fernandez.

"Better gather up those bolts and put them in your pocket," the engineer directed Fernandez.

"Got them."

Johnson rubbed his bald spot as he waited for the two men to do his bidding, then took the flashlight Cox handed to him. "Let's have a look at what we have in here." He switched on his flashlight and stepped into the dark hole left by the removal of the plate, entering the huge steel chamber of the boiler.

He flicked the flashlight around the damp interior for a few moments as his two helpers scrambled into the hole behind him and then spoke, his voice echoing off the metal walls. "Fernandez, you check the sensors, over there." He motioned with the beam of his light. "Cox, you come with me and let's see if we can see anything wrong with the tubes feeding the turbines. And everyone be careful. Just because we sprayed the inside to cool it down doesn't mean there won't be hot spots."

"Yes, sir," both men said in unison, their voices eerily loud in the steel room.

Johnson flicked the beam of his light ahead of him, then stopped and quickly studied the main weld running up the side of the chamber. Of course it couldn't be that, the engineer chided himself after he'd done his hasty inspection of the seam. A leak there would cause the pressure to drop, not build up. Besides, the work crew they'd hired at Manila had done repair work in here just a couple of weeks ago. They undoubtedly had inspected all the seams then.

On the other hand, he did need to be thorough. Something was wrong, and it didn't hurt to check everything while they were at it. His thoughts returned to the task at hand as he came to rungs welded to the inside of the boiler. "Hold your light on the ladder while I climb up," he ordered Cox.

The engineer clamped his own light onto his tool belt while Cox shone his beam on the steel rungs. Johnson started his ascent, carefully touching each rung before he latched onto it, to be sure it wasn't too hot. As he climbed, his shadow flickered like a giant bat fluttering on the curved metal ceiling high above him. His boots squeaked and reverberated off the rungs.

Somewhere in the dark chamber, water slowly dripped into one of the many tiny pools covering the bottom, making the huge steel drum seem more like a cave than the bowels of the boiler. Johnson made a mental note to himself to check the dripping later if he didn't find anything in the tubes.

He reached the top and carefully locked his arm through the uppermost rung so he wouldn't be dislodged by the pitching of the ship; then he retrieved his flashlight with his free hand.

"Shall I come up?" Cox asked from below him.

"No," Johnson answered. "There's hardly room for me up here." The engineer smiled to himself, imagining what it would be like if he'd ordered Cox up the ladder. For a moment the swaying inside the darkened chamber caused the engineer to feel dizzy; then the sensation passed as he flicked on his flashlight and could again see what was around him.

Johnson shone the beam down one of the foot-wide mouths of pipes that, along with similar tubes coming from the aft boiler, diverted steam toward

the turbines, supplying power to run the pro-
pellers as well as the generators that created elec-
tricity for the ship.

Everything looked normal, the burnished stainless steel gleaming in the light as the beam traversed it. He leaned over to the second tube and
shone the beam down it.

"What the—" Johnson muttered, his surprise
evident as he peered down the tube. For a moment
his eyes refused to focus on where he was looking.
Then he realized the beam wasn't revealing a shadow or a corroded spot on the inside of the pipe but
rather an actual object. "What the—" he repeated,
unaware of what he was saying. He continued
studying the section of pipe, trying to decide just
what it was he saw.

"You find something?" Cox's voice called from
below, startling the engineer.

"Sure have," Johnson answered, finally realizing what he was seeing. "It's no wonder the boiler
isn't working right."

The engineer reached into the tube, but the
wet mass of cloth, hair, and tiny bones was out of
his reach. Johnson pulled his hand out, feeling as if
it were fouled with the plague, even though he
knew the steam that had baked and matted the
material had also undoubtedly sterilized it. He
clung to the rung as the ship reeled from the blow
of another heavy wave.

"What's up there?" Cox inquired.

"Quite literally a rat's nest."

"A what?"

"Remember when they overhauled this boiler

two weeks ago in Manila and they replaced the rusted-out section along the bottom of this chamber?"

"Yeah. Did they leave something behind that got clogged in the tubes?"

"Not exactly. But while they were working down where you are, a mother rat was up here building a nest with all the rags she could find to drag up here along with her brood."

"But wouldn't the steam—"

"Kill them? It sure would and it sure did. We're going to have some real work ahead of us getting these blasted rats scraped off the inside of the boiler tubes."

"What's the radar pinging off of?" Captain Edmonton asked, checking the map in front of him. The trace on the scope showed something big, dead ahead of them. At first they had thought it was another ship, but then they had realized that the sheer size and distance could only mean it was an island.

But there wasn't such a spot on the chart.

Abruptly the port hatch opened, letting in a burst of cold air. A soaked crewman stamped the water off his feet as he secured the door and then threw his hat on the floor in his haste to get the plastic-covered package he carried across the deck and into the captain's hand. "I think I got the right maps, sir," Zellerman said as the officer took the wet container from him.

"Great, let's have a look," Edmonton said, ripping open the plastic bag of maps that the crewman had retrieved from the chart room. The officer carefully placed them onto the table in front of him; despite the plastic covering, the maps had become damp, and Edmonton unrolled them carefully to keep from tearing them.

Zellerman dropped his rain gear to the floor and helped the captain spread out the maps over the one they'd been using, carefully placing the new charts into the table clamps to keep them from rolling back up.

The captain ran his finger over the top chart, quickly orienting himself and then finding their position. He traced their heading until his finger came to a flyspecklike mark on the page. "There it is," he said, tapping the spot with his finger. "Too tiny and out of the way to even be included on the large map we normally use." He squinted at the tiny print beside the dot. "Kakira," he read. "That's the name of the little piece of rock dead ahead of us. Kakira."

"Shall I plot a course to take us around it?" Zellerman asked, looking at the map.

"No, I've got a better idea," the captain replied, stroking his chin. He turned toward his navigator. "I think maybe our luck is changing."

7

The MH-60K raced the storm, nearly out of control as it bucked the cross winds that were swept ahead of the approaching typhoon. From time to time the helicopter seemed to stall in the air when powerful gusts crashed into its nose, decelerating the machine so suddenly it jerked the crew and passengers forward as if they'd hit an invisible barrier.

"I hope we hang together," Oz muttered, aware that the helicopter had been overdesigned, but wondering if they weren't exceeding its limits. "How's everything holding up back there, O.T.?"

"Some loose junk is cascading around on the floor and one sailor is sick, but otherwise we're okay."

"You know things are bad when sailors are sea-sick," Death Song quipped, tapping buttons along the HSD screen to update the plotting of the course they were taking back to the U.S. Navy air-craft carrier.

Another blast ripped at the ship, nearly caus-ing Oz to bite his tongue as the chopper was thrown sideways and seemed to hang in the air before regaining its forward momentum. "How far now?"

"We're ten kilometers from the *Kitty Hawk* and closing," Death Song replied. "Fuel's going to be the problem. We're burning up our reserves in a hurry."

Oz glanced at the display. "Yeah, our engines are maxed bucking this wind."

"What are we going to do for a cable when we go in?" Death Song asked, glancing toward the pilot.

"I've been wondering about that myself. With the winch shot we're going to have some problems. That deck's going to be dancing around in these waves. And we sure as hell aren't going to be able to thread the belts through our winch. Have to worry about that when we get there, I guess."

Minutes later Death Song warned the pilot: "We've nearly exhausted our emergency reserves. And we're still about nine kilometers from the ship. Closing slowly."

Oz clicked on his radio. "CV-63, this is NS-1. We're nine kilometers north of you and nearly out of fuel. Requesting permission to proceed directly to your helideck. Over."

Static answered his message and then the radio became silent.

"CV-63," the pilot called. "Please repeat message."

"We repeat," the radioman on the *Kitty Hawk* said. "Proceed to helideck. We'll keep the whole deck clear for you in case you can't set down there. Our deck crew is standing by. Do you need medical assistance upon arrival. Over."

"Negative on the medical. Everyone is mobile. You might have a team ready to fish us out if we don't make the deck—we're running on fumes now. Over."

"I'm sorry, NS-1, but we can't get a rescue team out in this. Better keep on coming in and don't fool around out there. I've already got a team ready to secure your cable to the deck. Over."

"Negative on the cable team," Oz radioed back. "Our winch is shot. I'm going to have to stake us in place the hard way. Over."

There was no reply for a moment and then the radioman on the *Kitty Hawk* replied in a low voice, "Good luck, NS-1. Over and out."

"Didn't sound too positive," Oz remarked, flipping off the radio. He remained silent for a few minutes as the distance to the ship diminished. "Death Song, I can see we're as good as out of fuel. But do you have any idea just how much is left in the tanks?"

"Can't tell. We're empty as far as the gauges go. Four kilometers to the ship."

An alarm started beeping, warning the pilot that he was out of fuel.

"Kill the alarm," Oz ordered and glanced at the VSD screen. Just three and a half kilometers to go. The aircraft shook with the wind, and Oz waited to hear the sputtering of the engines; if that occurred, the rotors would automatically revert to the position that would allow autorotation, safely lowering them to the ground. Only this time there was no ground below them, only water.

And I haven't been good enough lately to walk on water, the pilot thought grimly.

"We're almost there!" Death Song proclaimed as they inched toward the ship, barely visible through the rain. "Keep going, baby."

With the head wind shoving the chopper backward, the MH-60K torpidly advanced to the edge of the deck, and then they were over the reeling surface that rolled with the waves. The engines sputtered, missing and then starting again for a moment before losing power. Abruptly the helicopter dropped and then, as the wind caught it, flopped backward, retreating toward the edge of the flight deck.

Oz shoved at the collective pitch lever, causing the MH-60K to drop as quickly as possible. The pilot pushed the column forward, kicking the rudder pedal to align the nose of the helicopter with the ship. The aircraft slammed against the hard steel surface, bouncing on its landing struts and wheels, then rolling toward the edge of the deck below the tail of the helicopter. The wind continued to shove them over the edge as the pilot rapidly hit the brakes, locking the wheels.

"O.T., Luger," Oz called over the intercom. "Get our passengers off at once. I'm not sure how long I can keep us on the deck."

"Opening the side doors now, sir," O.T. answered.

The helicopter shook and rattled as the gale buffeted it. The sailors inside the MH-60K quickly exited, bent nearly double or crawling to keep from being blown off the deck by the high wind that engulfed them.

Deck hands with ropes tied around their waists staggered toward the helicopter that oscillated in the squall, lightning flashing to silhouette it against the black sky. Some of the deck hands guided the sailors coming from the helicopter to safety while others held onto the chopper in an effort to keep it from being blown off the deck.

The *Kitty Hawk* lurched with the slap of a wave, and the helicopter scooted toward the edge of the air strip. The sailors rapidly attached a heavy cable to the large cable hook below the chopper, which now teetered near the edge of the deck. The seamen labored swiftly and silently, since the noise of the storm made conversation impossible.

Within seconds the line was secure; one of the sailors signaled and the winch at its other end was activated, pulling the helicopter toward the safety of the nearest elevator.

Oz let out a sigh of relief. His earphones crackled with a close lightning strike, and then the *Kitty Hawk's* radioman called to him. "Can you guide your chopper toward the elevator, NS-1?"

"That's a roger, CV-63. Boy am I glad to finally be tethered down."

"Can't have you blowing over the side, can we? Hang on and we'll have you safe and sound in a jiffy."

Within five minutes the chopper was on the elevator, and deck hands rushed through the downpour to get blocks into place on either side of its wheels to help keep it from rolling. The section of the deck where the craft rested quickly dropped downward, revealing the hangar below the upper surface of the ship.

"Looks like we actually made it," Oz said as they reached the first level below deck.

Sailors scampered around the chopper and shoved it into the safety of the hangar.

"Luger and O.T.," the pilot called as he guided the wheels of the chopper toward their berth. "Get everything squared away back there while we go through the postflight checklist up here."

"Captain," Luger's voice came over the intercom. "I think you'd better exempt O.T. from the work. His hands are cut to ribbons."

"Better report to sick bay, O.T.," Oz said.

"I'm okay, sir. Just a few little scratches—"

"That's an order," Oz interrupted. "I can't afford to have my warrant officer down any extra time because he tried to prove how macho he was and got his wounds infected."

"Right, sir," O.T. said meekly. "I don't want anyone to think I'm too tough."

Oz shook his head as Luger chuckled into the intercom. "Let's get on with it," the pilot ordered Death Song, who commenced reading from the postflight checklist.

Major Yoshiro Tashida stood naked with eyes closed, balanced on a slab of ancient lava at the top of the cliff. Being the highest spot on the island, it was also the holiest simply because it was closest to the sun. The wind threw heavy droplets of rain against Tashida's bare face and soaked his hair until it clung to his head in a gray mat. The lightning etched patterns through his eyelids, and the thunder rocked the island, almost hurting his ears with its intensity.

The forces of Shinto, the way of the gods, are powerful tonight, he told himself. The *kami*, the gods in the most basic forces of rivers, rocks, and—now—the storm, invigorated him. The elements also returned his mind to the divine storm of his personal god, the warrior spirit Hachiman, which had swept the Pacific so long ago when Japan had finally asserted its strength to the world.

Tonight he was his own priest, his own *kannushi-san*. The State Shintoism stressed patriotism and the divine origins of the emperor, Hirohito, the offspring of the sun goddess who created *Nippon*. Japan was the gateway of the sun. But tonight the *kami* of Hachiman ruled the storm that invigorated Tashida as he stood his ground to the driving wind and rain. Standing there, he proved to his god that he and his island were strong enough to withstand any punishment that was sent their way.

"We are ready for each and every *bakyaro* the Americans choose to send against us," he called to the tempest. "Now send their armies so we can fully prove ourselves. Test us. Blow them here, god of wind and storms."

He had prayed similar prayers before to no avail. But tonight, in the squall that thrashed his island, he felt his prayer might finally be answered. Perhaps he would at long last have a chance to face the American soldiers instead of the fools and spies that trickled to him with their strange radios, gadgets, and absurd clothes.

Tashida stretched out his arms in supplication to his gods, and the lightning flashed, revealing the swaying palms far below him, their fronds twisted and broken by the gale sweeping the island. He smiled in the abrupt darkness that left ghost images dancing on his retinas.

The major hoped he would soon have a chance to demonstrate the fighting prowess of the ancient *Bushido* like his kinsmen who had done so in the centuries before. "Soon," he pleaded to the wind of the *kami*. "Let them come soon."

The thunder seemed to rattle a rejoinder.

Yet he was unsure. "Please. Very soon."

Tashida's eyes narrowed as he looked toward the ocean. A growing light floated over the heaving sea, bobbing up and down and vanishing from time to time only to reappear as he watched. At first, he thought he was seeing the afterimage of the lightning. But the light grew and gradually became groups of smaller lights.

A ship, he realized.

A monstrous ship, from the looks of it. One full of American soldiers, perhaps. He hoped it would be soldiers rather than more of the stupid spies who begged and pleaded and told nothing even when tortured beyond the limits of their bodies.

He studied the lights a moment more, smiled, and turned to pick his way down the steep path.

"How accurate is that map?" Captain Edmonton asked his navigator. He thought the chart was so old and frayed, it looked like something Captain Kidd had carried in his hip pocket.

"It should be pretty accurate," Zellerman answered. "It was printed in 1958 before they had satellites, but the General Map Company has always been noted for its—"

"All right, all right," Edmonton snapped. "We don't have much time. I just don't want to be running aground on a coral reef or something that isn't on the map. So this course looks like the best to take us to the lee side of the island?"

"Yes, Captain. Once we get around it, the shallows here should break up the waves, while this area is deep enough for us even in low tide. We couldn't ask for a better port to weather the storm."

"All right, give the helmsman the coordinates. Stay next to me on the bridge to double check my orders—we won't have time to maneuver around if we make any mistakes. Not with only half power as our maximum."

"Aye, Captain," Zellerman answered.

The captain took a deep breath and tried to control his fear. It was going to be tricky steering through the narrow channel on the near side of the island. But it won't be any tricker than turning around in the storm, he decided. He had done that and got them through in one piece. Maybe his luck would hold.

He took another deep breath and tried to relax.

"We're approaching the channel, Captain," the navigator called. "It's time to start maneuvering."

Edmonton scanned the chart one more time. "Sonar, if we're in danger of running aground, I want you to sing out. Otherwise stay quiet."

"Aye, Captain."

The officer checked the radar scope. "What's the range to the island?"

"One point two kilometers."

"Left one degree," Edmonton ordered, glancing toward Zellerman, who gave a barely perceptible nod of approval.

"Left one degree," the helmsman echoed, shifting the wheel ever so slightly and keeping his eye on the compass.

"Radar, call out our range in tenth-of-a-kilometer increments," Edmonton commanded.

"Aye, Captain. One point one."

The bridge was silent except for the wind battering the ship.

"Captain, we're running out of elbow room down there," the sonar man called. "Think you better take a look!"

Edmonton whirled toward the sonar screen and saw a mountainlike projection coming off the floor of the ocean, right in their path.

"Looks like a sunken ship," the sonar man said.

"Full left rudder," the captain ordered, trying to remain calm.

"Full left rudder," the helmsman repeated.

The ship listed to starboard as the wind caught it on the side. Edmonton gritted his teeth and held the brass rail, wishing he'd been able to use his ballast tanks to stabilize their turn and hoping they'd acted in time. It was hard to be sure with the wind constantly shoving them forward.

He glanced back at the sonar. They had made it past the wreck. "Right full rudder."

"Right full rudder," the helmsman said.

"One click to the shore," the radarman called.

"Straighten us out," the captain ordered. As the helmsman carried out the command, Edmonton checked the sonar, the map, and then the radar. "Right one degree."

"Right one degree."

The captain straightened up and let out his breath. Barring any more sunken wrecks, it should be clear passage to the lee side of the island from here on. Then they'd be home free.

The fact started to sink in. They were almost home free.

Maybe tomorrow I can even make things up with my sick passengers and tour guides, he thought with a smile. *They'll have their very own desert island to explore while Johnson gets our boiler back on line.*

"Ahhhh," Luger said as the medic inserted the tongue depressor into the airman's mouth and inspected the airman's tonsils.

"You say you often get airsick?"

"'eth, thur," Luger answered around the tongue depressor. "But only when I can't see outside the plane," he added after the wooden stick was removed.

"So you don't have any problem on a copter." The medic nodded. "I was wondering how you could work if you got airsick all the time." The doctor pressed the release on the wastebasket with his foot so the lid popped open. "Well, it looks like you have seasickness to contend with right now. But while you're in here, let me check your eyes and ears," he said, tossing the tongue depressor into the open trash container. "I bet you guys don't have physicals except when you reenlist."

"No, sir," the airman replied, "I guess we don't." He watched the doctor out of the corner of his eye as the man inserted an otoscope into his ear.

The doctor studied the ear drum and canal a moment. "It always amazes me how the army cares for its personnel. I bet they inspect your copters every time they come in. But the guys manning those million-dollar machines don't get a second glance unless they're obviously injured. Let's check your other ear." The doctor was silent as he examined the airman. "Well, your ears are okay, too," he finally said. "Looks like a little Dramamine should have you shipshape in no time—pun intended."

"That would be good, sir," Luger nodded, blanching as the ship lurched with another wave.

The doctor crossed to a metal cabinet and unlocked it. "If it's any consolation, the report is that the worst of the storm should be past in a few hours. The waves will let up in a day or so."

The medic took a small bottle of scored yellow tablets out of the cabinet and handed the vial to Luger. "Just follow the instructions on the bottle—take one every four hours. I'd ground you if you were flying a chopper, but you're a gunner, right?"

"Yes, sir."

"You should be okay then. But warn your commanding officer that these may make you a little drowsy. You're not taking any antibiotics, are you? That might create a problem."

"No, sir."

"Good. Antibiotics interact with this Dramamine. But other than your motion sickness, you're in good shape. Your blood pressure is normal and your throat and ears look good. I'd take a blood and urine sample but you'd probably be gone before we got the results."

"That's okay, sir."

"Well then, good luck, soldier."

"Thanks, sir," the airman said, saluting and struggling not to throw up on the talkative medic.

Oz could have practically located the mess hall by the tantalizing smells wafting down the swaying passageway on the mid-decks of the *Kitty Hawk*. The murmur of hundreds of talking and laughing sailors became louder as he entered the massive, low-ceilinged mess hall.

After selecting one of the metal trays and sliding it along the stainless steel counter, he directed the cook behind the counter to place a steak patty and scoop of mashed potatoes onto his plate and cover both with rich brown gravy. A roll, tossed salad, and steaming cup of black coffee completed his meal.

He carried the tray toward the table where the other crews of the four Night Stalkers helicopters sat, conspicuous in their army battle dress uniforms.

Oz set the tray down, eyeing the mug that threatened to slosh coffee over the rim as the ship lurched beneath them.

"How's Luger?" O.T. asked Oz around a large mouthful of cinnamon roll.

"Yeah, he was looking pretty bad when we left him," Death Song added.

"Still looking green," Oz grinned, easing himself into the backless bench that ran down the side of the long table. "Doesn't look like the storm's hurt your appetites any."

"Bet Luger'll be glad when this storm dies down and we can head home," Death Song remarked, scooting down the bench to make more room for Oz.

"Now that's the understatement of the week," O.T. joshed. "How soon *are* we going to get off this ship, anyway? I'm getting antsy myself, cooped up like this below decks."

"Sounds like the worst of the storm is already past," Oz said, breaking open the small plastic container of salad dressing and pouring it over his salad. "Word is, we should be able to leave for Andersen Air Force Base within twenty-four hours. Guam missed the brunt of the storm, so the air strip's in pretty good shape there."

"All right," O.T. exulted. "And then a cargo plane back to the good old U.S. of A."

The wind speed dropped as the *Pleasure Run* reached the lee side of the island; the mammoth waves that had crashed against the ship's forecastle and swept across the deck were dissipated by the mass of the island, so the upper decks were again safe for crewmen to walk across.

Captain Edmonton checked the compass to verify their heading. "How's it look, sonar?"

"Still only ten meters under our keel."

Edmonton swore under his breath. The chart had been wrong about the depth of the ocean on the lee side of the island. Now they were in danger of going aground; they would for sure if the waves got any higher.

"Hang on," the sonar officer cautioned. "It's dropping off again. Now we have twenty meters under our keel."

The captain and the others on the bridge waited tensely for the next reading.

"Thirty meters. Still dropping."

"Radar, how far to shore?" Edmonton asked, steadying himself against the brass rail on the wall.

"About one kilometer, sir."

The captain knew that the ocean bottom was still close to the ship, but since it was low tide, and the wind was dying down, it shouldn't present any problem. This is as good a place as any to anchor, he decided. "Full stop."

"Full stop," the helmsman repeated.

"Drop anchors."

"Dropping anchors."

Edmonton checked his watch and turned to the radar technician, who was studying the glowing screen in front of him. "Any company?"

"No, Captain. Just the island."

Rain spattered on the glass viewing ports as Edmonton stared toward the land mass, which was hidden by the heavy rain and darkness. With any luck, the island would be worth visiting for his passengers, though getting in close enough to ferry many of them over and back would be tough and likely a logistical nightmare for the cruise director. But that's his problem, the captain added to himself.

According to everything Zellerman could find

on the ship's maps, the out-of-the-way island had been uninhabited since World War II and possibly even before then. A little exploring on Kakira should keep the tourists busy and happy, hopefully, while engineering cleans out the tubes in the forward boiler, he mused.

"Full stop and anchors are lowered, Captain."

"Let's shut off some of the lights. Won't need to warn anybody of our approach now that we're dead in the water."

"Aye, sir."

Edmonton yawned as he turned back from the port. "Now if engineering can clean up the forward boiler, we should be in good shape."

"Aye, sir," the helmsman said with a chuckle.

A rat's nest, the captain thought, shaking his head and rubbing his tired neck while recalling how the ship had nearly gone down because some furry creature had sneaked aboard and clogged up a boiler tube with rags. Murphy's law prevails. But they had made it to a safe harbor and with any luck would be on their way by this time tomorrow.

"Just got an updated weather report, Captain," the radioman announced.

"What have you got?"

"Sounds like the storm's headed northwest. We should be pretty much out of it by tomorrow."

"Good." Edmonton smiled wearily, turning from the radio post. "I'm going to my cabin," he told the crew on the bridge. "Call me if anything changes. Mr. Zellerman, you have the bridge for the rest of this watch."

"Aye, Captain."

* * *

Lieutenant Noboru Ishimoto watched the ship anchored in the harbor through the binoculars taken from the American boat captured two days earlier. The optics gathered enough light that he could see the ship well before it doused its lights.

Why did they come into the harbor with their lights on? he wondered, lowering the lens marked "Made in Japan." The lieutenant puzzled over what kind of madness motivated the Americans to label their optical systems with such characters.

Probably our translator is mistaken about what the markings say, the officer reflected, lifting the binoculars to his eyes once more and studying the ship in the harbor. It didn't appear the vessel was going to turn all its lights back on, though several jewels of electric illumination still glistened from ports, along with the vessel's navigational lights.

How long has it been since I last saw an electric light? Ishimoto wondered, lowering the binoculars again and retrieving the cleaning cloth from its case. Holding the cloth in his wrinkled hands, he carefully wiped the lens free of the drops that managed to get through the thick foliage around him.

He replaced the lens cloth into the case along with the binoculars before turning toward his messenger, who waited quietly beside him in the darkness. "Go tell Major Tashida that the ship appears to have anchored in the harbor and has now shut off some, but not all, of its lights."

"*Hai,*" the private said and then rose, turned, and melted into the vegetation behind Ishimoto.

The old lieutenant studied the vessel that was barely discernible to the naked eye and wondered what the men on the ship were up to. Major Tashida thought the vessel might be a decoy to capture the Japanese soldiers' attention while an attack was mounted against the other side of the island. That seemed possible, though it was hard for Ishimoto to understand why an attack wasn't simply mounted without any warning. The Americans were known for their surprise attacks; coming in unannounced would have achieved the element of surprise that Western armies seemed to value so highly.

One thing is sure, Ishimoto thought, crouching in the darkness and wishing the trees above him afforded better protection from the rain. *Things will be changing on the island now that the ship has arrived.*

In fact, things were already changing. Since the major had sighted the ship, the talk among Ishimoto's men had been about how they would destroy the Americans if they approached the island. Now that the tiger was at the doorstep, all the young men were growing silent.

And this is only the beginning, he mused, pulling his tattered handwoven collar up around his neck.

10

Oz led the four Night Stalkers flight teams onto the flight deck at midnight. The fliers filed toward their helicopters, positioned on the port extension of the *Kitty Hawk's* flight deck, which stretched nearly 350 yards from stem to stern. The steel deck rolled under Oz's feet, the waves in the aftermath of the storm continuing to rock the huge ship. The overcast sky now only hinted at the tempest that had passed.

"I hate getting out in the middle of the night like this," O.T. yelled over the thunder of an F-4 Phantom that raced along the deck. Propelled by the powerful steam catapult that threw it off the runway, the plane's afterburners glowed in the dim light.

"Orders are orders," Oz yelled back, pausing to inspect the MH-60K before climbing into the side door of the cockpit. Instead of the usual weapons pods, the aircraft's modified external tank suite struts carried large fuel canisters that were connected directly into the aircraft's fuel lines; the external tank system, or ETS, had been developed for a sister helicopter, the HH-60D Night Hawk, and incorporated into the MH-60 SOA helicopter. With the ETS, the helicopter had a ferry range of 2,220 kilometers, more than enough to reach Guam from the *Kitty Hawk*.

The pilot reflected on how he always felt a little naked without the usual armament of missiles and machine-gun pod on the struts, though both side gunners on each chopper still had their 7.62-mm Miniguns and each crewman had his personal weapons as well, usually a handgun and often a carbine and knife. *And the chances of running into trouble are practically nil anyway,* Oz tried to reassure himself.

But he still felt vulnerable as he donned his helmet and climbed into the chopper.

After stowing his PK-15 submachine gun in its carrier behind his seat, he snapped the cord running from his helmet into the intercom system. "How are you doing, Luger?"

"I don't feel sick but I am pretty drowsy, sir."

"You can nap on this flight. After we get into the air, why don't you go back to the passenger compartment and relax. Things should be pretty tame on this outing."

"Thanks, sir. I think I'll take you up on that."

"Death Song," the pilot said, turning toward his navigator. "Let's get this bird wound up."

"Roger, Captain," the Native American answered. "We're all anxious to get back into the air."

Oz snapped open a tiny pocket on his flight vest, extracted a key, and jabbed it into the panel lock. Twisting the lock to ON, he commenced the procedures necessary to get them into the air, checking that the power levers were back to their OFF position, the master ignition set to ON, and the engine start switch to OFF. The pilot toggled switches ENG 1 and ENG 2. "Start the APU," he instructed his navigator.

Death Song flipped the auxiliary power unit's BATT switch on and pressed the MASTER CAUTION button, lighting the Chiclet panel that showed the onboard computer was checking its systems.

Oz checked the panel as Death Song activated the auxiliary power unit by slipping its control to RUN, then flipping it to START and releasing it. The APU's turbine hummed to life, supplying the energy to power the hydraulics and start the engines.

The pilot released the rotor brake, set both power levers from their OFF positions to IDLE, and held in the ENG START button for engine number one. The engine behind him coughed to a start, its pitch quickly smoothing out to a deep hum. As he started the second engine, he twisted in his bucket seat to check the progress of the helicopters behind him. One by one their blades starting twisting, creating a low-pitched, furious thumping.

Oz clicked on the radio, which was set to the short-range UHF battle-net channel used to communicate between the helicopters. "NS Pack, this is NS-1. How're you guys doing back there?"

"NS-1, Two is prepared to get off this floating tin can. Over."

"Ditto for NS-3," the pilot of the third chopper responded.

"NS-4 is ready."

"Stand by for my signal," Oz told them and

then switched the radio to the CAN frequency. "This is NS-1 requesting clearance for my party of four army jocks to take off."

"NS-1," the air boss on the USS *Kitty Hawk* replied. "You're cleared for takeoff. Have a good flight to gooney-bird land."

"Thanks, CV-63." Oz shifted back to his ABN frequency, lowering and adjusting the night vision goggles on his helmet as he spoke. "We'll use a diamond formation," he called. "Two to starboard and Three to port. Four will bring up the rear. One is lifting in five seconds. Over and out."

Silently counting to five, the pilot smashed the throttles into FLY, making the chopper's engines whine to full power, rotors churning and engines belching a small cloud of smoke as they increased their speed. Lifting the collective pitch lever coupled to the throttles, Oz raised the chopper from the deck. Then he pushed the control column forward, causing the MH-60K to nose down and hurtle forward over the surging ocean.

The chopper dropped toward the water's surface as the aircraft left the ground-effect upblast from the deck, and the pilot compensated by raising the collective pitch lever. The MH-60K rose above the ocean like a black hornet. Oz kicked his left rudder pedal and wheeled the chopper onto its course heading; behind him the other three helicopters gracefully mimicked the lead chopper's actions and fell into their diamond formation.

Oz quickly glanced over the displays in front of him. Everything looked good. He checked his watch. Twenty-four hundred hours, he thought, doing a quick mental calculation. That would make it about seven in the morning at Fort Bragg; Commander Warner probably wouldn't be in yet. So he'd have to leave a message for the officer. "Death Song, connect us to the COMSAT so we can let the base know we're headed for Guam."

"Just a minute," the navigator said, activating the computer controls that uplinked to the military communications satellite high above them. Within moments the two devices had given the proper electronic "handshakes" and the MH-60K's radio signal was connected to their home base at Fort Bragg, North Carolina.

"How are you, NS-1?" the army officer in the United States called. "Hear things have been pretty rocky out there. Over."

"That they have," Oz replied. "We're all in good shape. I've got four birds leaving for our next destination. ETA is in five to six hours, depending on the wind speed we have to buck."

"All right, NS-1. I'll leave a message for Mother Hen. Your C-5As and the rest of the contingent you left behind before starting your mission are on schedule. They'll be reaching the base about six hours after you arrive. Then home again, home again, jiggety jig."

"Sounds good. NS-1 over and out."

Death Song unlinked the radio. "Just one thousand, five hundred, sixty-three kilometers to go."

"Remind me to laugh when we get there," Oz said, shoving the control column forward to bring them to near-maximum speed of 290 kilometers per hour. "I think Luger has the right idea for this trip," the pilot added, glancing down at the dark waves that seemed to race past the four army helicopters as they hurtled through the night sky.

Five and a half hours after they had left the *Kitty Hawk,* the small convoy of Army helicopters received clearance from Andersen Air Force Base to land on their strip at the northern end of Guam. The lights of the villages and small cities on the twenty-mile-long island glowed faintly on the southern horizon as the MH-60Ks came in low and set down on the blacktop runway surfaced with white shells.

After shutting down his helicopter and checking to be sure an Air Force security team was in place around the perimeter of the aircraft, Oz and his men headed toward their assigned barracks.

"That breeze feels good," O.T. said, staring toward the sky, his boots clicking against the hard tarmac. "Look at the stars around here. If we weren't at sea level, I'd swear they were closer to the earth than they are in the States."

"There's no light pollution," Death Song said. "There aren't that many bright lights around here, so you can see more stars. Man, I could stay out here all night just looking up at the sky."

"You guys can watch the stars if you want," Oz told his men. "I'm going to get a hot shower and hit the hay. And there's no rush to get around tomorrow; anyone waking me before noon will face a firing squad."

"Are you suggesting we sleep late tomorrow?" O.T. asked.

"You got it," Oz replied. "It's going to be a slow day by the time the ground crews get the choppers broken down and loaded into the cargo planes with the rest of the choppers we left behind."

"Hurry up and wait," Death Song nodded, suppressing a yawn.

"Hey, you guys aren't sleepy, are you?" Luger said. "Heck, I'm wide awake now."

"Don't expect us to keep you company," O.T. told him. "Just because you snored all the way to Guam doesn't mean the rest of us aren't worn out."

11

Captain Edmonton studied the yellowed chart Zellerman had stretched across the map table. "Where in the world do you get all these old maps?" he asked his navigator.

"Auctions, sales . . . I guess I kind of collect these things."

"Well, your hobby's paid off this trip. So you think we might be able to go on into the harbor—if this map's correct."

"Yes, sir. See how this channel runs right up almost to the beach? I bet we could get within maybe a hundred yards of the shore." Zellerman looked out the starboard port and pointed at Kakira. "Looks like some type of volcanic action lifted this section of the island and created a natural harbor suited for large ships like ours."

"So what's bugging you?" the captain asked. "I've seen that expression before."

"Well, the catch is that the survey for the map was taken in 1922. A lot of sediment could have washed into the bay since then."

Edmonton rubbed his clean-shaven chin a

moment before speaking. "Let's go ahead and give it a shot." He turned, studying the shore that was shrouded in mists under the overcast morning sky. "If we go in slowly, sonar can keep us out of trouble. Take a careful look at the shore to be sure we're heading in at the right point. And then let's ease toward Kakira and see what secrets she's been keeping all these years."

"Yes, sir."

"All right, gentlemen," the captain addressed the sailors manning the bridge. "We're going to head toward the island in a few minutes. Stay alert, and we'll see how close we can get to shore without running aground. I'm sure our passengers would like to get out and explore the island, and the closer we are to it, the less time we'll have to spend ferrying them back and forth on our launches."

Zellerman's old map proved to be accurate. By ten o'clock the sun had broken through the clouds, and the *Pleasure Run* was anchored only three hundred yards offshore.

Passenger Dan Brooks stood in one of the ship's launches, holding out his hand to steady his wife, Mary, as she cautiously stepped into the boat that rocked alongside the ship.

"I hope I'm not going to get sick again," she said, eyeing the water as she settled into the damp seat next to her husband.

"You'll be okay," Dan replied as they squeezed into a pair of narrow plastic seats. "Just keep your eyes on the shore over there. We're going to be leaving for the island in a couple of minutes. The boat's almost full. You'll have sand under your feet in no time."

Mary watched the last couple climb into the boat and then looked toward the shoreline. One of the launches was returning, leaving a group of waving passengers behind on the pristine beach. "Looks like the island they found King Kong on," Mary said.

"Yeah, it kind of does," Dan laughed. "One thing you have to admit, if we'd been looking for adventure, this trip would have given us our money's worth."

"As I recall, you said, 'Let's take a nice relaxing cruise.' That was what you suggested."

"Yeah, and you're not going to let me forget this trip was my idea, are you?"

"How else can I browbeat you into another vacation next year?"

"You've got a point." He chuckled.

The burly sailor sitting at the controls of the small boat started up its engine; the racket of the motor made further conversation difficult. Mary gripped Dan's hand tightly as they pulled away from the ship.

He smiled at her and patted her hand. "Just a few more minutes and we'll be there," he yelled.

The Japanese soldier signaled from across the ridge to Lieutenant Ishimoto. "Another group of Americans is coming up the ridge," he told the riflemen lying on the damp ground around him.

"Remember, shoot only if one of them is about to escape from our people on the ground." The soldiers hidden in the brush below the lieutenant had silently captured or killed all the Americans in the previous groups, working swiftly with swords and bayonets.

So far the troops had succeeded in dealing with five of the groups without alerting the others on the beach or the distant ship. Best of all, the riflemen Ishimoto was overseeing hadn't wasted any of the precious few cartridges the Japanese still had left.

"Don't shoot unless you have to," the lieutenant warned, looking directly at the young soldier who gripped his Type 99 bolt-action rifle so tightly in his shaky hands that his knuckles turned white.

Young and inexperienced, Ishimoto thought, turning to observe the path the Americans would likely be coming up. And now he's scared. The private who had bragged the most a week ago about killing Americans was now the shakiest of the lot. The old lieutenant was not so sure how well the troops on the island would do against the Americans, who might have seen many battles during the long war that had now stretched over decades.

Of course the Americans his men had been capturing today weren't soldiers. None were armed with more than a pocket knife, and all were dressed in the same type of gaudy clothing as the other spies the Japanese had captured over the last few years. What are these impure invaders doing here? he wondered.

He had been present when Major Tashida had tortured the spies from the earlier boats that had arrived at the island; the major never learned anything about why the spies came or how the war was going. Ishimoto suspected the major engaged in the fruitless exercises more for pleasure than in order to gain information, for the more Americans Major Tashida sent to *Yomi-no-Kuni,* death's land of pollution, the less the inquisitor knew about these odd spies and their motives.

Now another band of the Americans slowly climbed the pathway, laughing and pointing toward the jungle like a band of sightseers. "Do not fire," the lieutenant warned his men again, looking directly at the young private whose hands were now shaking uncontrollably. "Keep your finger away from the trigger!" he hissed.

His warning came too late.

The bolt-action rifle the soldier held fired. Ishimoto whirled around to see how the Americans would react. They stood frozen on the trail, apparently unsure of what they'd heard.

Any moment they will flee, Ishimoto told himself. They would realize they were in danger and retreat. He had no choice. "Fire!"

His riflemen opened up on the people standing on the pathway, sending a deadly salvo of 7.7 mm bullets down the ridge.

As she raced with her husband toward the beach, putting distance between them and the gunmen on the ridge, Mary cried out, stumbled, and fell. Dan stopped and scooped her up in his as like he had when they'd first gotten married. Only now, instead of laughing, she was crying. He glanced down and saw why she'd fallen. He tore his eyes away from the oozing wound in her abdomen.

Watch the trail, he ordered himself, knowing that one misstep would mean a fall. Another volley of shots cracked past him, and three of the tourists ahead of him cried out and dropped, rolling down the hill like children's dolls. Dan leaped over a corpse that was missing the top of its head. The American tried not to gag as he stumbled on down the sandy trail.

"Get off the path!" he gasped to the remaining tourists running around him. *They won't be able to get a clear shot if we get off the trail,* he told himself, dashing into the foliage beside him.

The tall elephant grass cut his skin as he shoved through it, followed by three other tourists who came crashing into the foliage behind him as they all attempted to escape the gunmen on the ridge.

Dan stepped around the brush and was startled to see that a long trench had been dug into the hillside. He ran along its edge for a short distance and then came to a halt when a soldier with a rusty rifle leaped out of the brush in front of him, a long, wicked bayonet pointed directly at him and his wife.

The soldier spoke, and even though Dan couldn't understand what he said, his actions warned the Americans to stop.

Dan's mouth gaped open when he recognized the crudely woven uniform and the rifle the Japanese soldier carried. At first the American felt disoriented and then realized where his sense of déjà vu was coming from: he'd seen soldiers like this one in the Pacific before.

But that was during World War II.

"What the hell?" Dan asked as the soldier stepped forward, herding him toward the open trench. "Okay, buddy, keep your shirt on," the American said, carefully lowering himself and his injured wife.

"Take it easy," one of the other tourists cautioned as the Japanese soldier jabbed the blade toward him.

First one and then the next of the tourists dropped into the trench beside Dan and Mary. But the third tourist, a thin balding man whom Dan had never met, panicked and turned, crashing into the brush. The soldier moved with surprising rapidity, skewering the tourist. The green and blue Hawaiian shirt the man wore was rapidly stained crimson as the trooper jerked his blade out of his victim.

The tourist fell, crying in pain and trying to reach the wound on his back. The soldier rapidly jabbed with the long blade again and again until the man was dead.

The young trooper turned toward the other four tourists in the trench and motioned them forward.

Grimly, Dan led the way with his wife still in his arms, walking toward the mouth of a tunnel carved into the end of the long trench. The Americans said nothing as they entered the dark cavern, the soldier's eyes warning them that he would tolerate no more nonsense.

Captain Edmonton watched the tall waves rush toward the shore as another of the launches splashed through them, returning to the *Pleasure Run* to pick up the sixth group of passengers to ferry to the island. The sun glistened off the lush tropical vegetation of the island. "This is just like being alive again," he told the helmsman.

"Aye, sir."

The captain gazed over the aquamarine shallows that twinkled in the bright sunlight. A flock of gulls had already discovered the scraps the galley had tossed over the side and were fighting for the food. "Maybe we should scuttle the ship and settle down here with the natives—if there are any," the officer suggested, suppressing a grin when none of the crew in the bridge laughed or responded.

Edmonton remembered how it had been before he'd commanded a ship; except for the captain, no one on the bridge could afford to have a sense of humor. He crossed to the bulkhead, picked up the intercom phone, punched the button marked ENG.

The captain listened as the phone on the other end rang four times. "Engineering," Johnson's voice finally answered.

"How are things progressing with the boiler?"

"We're about done. It was a real sorry mess. If

that crud had gone into the turbines, I hate to think what would have happened."

"How's it look now?"

"There's no damage. My crew should have it up and running within three hours. But we won't be going anywhere for a while because we had to dismantle the tubes from both boilers where they lead to the turbines."

"That shouldn't be any problem," the captain replied. "In fact we—"

"Captain!" the helmsman interrupted.

"Hang on a minute," Edmonton told the engineer on the other end of the line. The officer turned to see why his conversation had been interrupted.

"Something's wrong out there," a breathless sailor reported through the hatchway. He pointed toward the shore. "We're hearing gun fire coming from the island."

"Probably someone just sneaked some fireworks to the island and is celebrating," the captain said, eyeing the crowd running along the beach. That did look odd to him, almost like a stampede; he snatched up the binoculars that hung around his neck and investigated the shoreline.

He watched the mob of passengers running toward the water. Some kind of game? he wondered.

Then he saw that several of the tourists fell, tumbling on the sand with such force that they undoubtedly were injured from the spills. The rest of the stampeding group finally reached the water, splashing furiously into it, waving at the ship as they struggled for deeper water. As the captain watched, great geysers erupted around the tourists and several more of the passengers dropped, floating facedown in the water.

Water that became bloodred.

"Holy Mother of God," Edmonton swore, swinging his binoculars toward the shoreline where he spotted the telltale flashing of muzzle blasts coming from the high ridge. "Someone *is* shooting at the passengers!"

The captain turned around with an oath and addressed the crewman who'd entered the bridge with the news of the gunfire. "Get the launches into the water and pick up as many of those poor devils as you can. If we hurry we might still save some of them."

"But the gunmen—"

"To hell with the gunmen; it's time to show a little courage, sailor."

"Aye, Captain," the nervous sailor mumbled. He turned and ran out the open hatchway.

"Captain," the helmsman cried. "There's a boat approaching us from the sea."

Edmonton swung toward the port and gazed at the white yacht speeding toward them. The machine gun mounted on its bow was unmistakable. "What the hell is going on?"

The captain tried to decide what to do. The engines were down because of the work on the boiler. It might take hours for them to be back on line. The ship was nearly defenseless, with only a handgun locked in the captain's safe. Fighting them off was unthinkable.

Or was it? He did have all kinds of weapons hidden in the forward storage hold. There'd be hell to pay later when the authorities learned about the ordnance, but that was a better alternative to being shot like the poor bastards on shore.

"Captain, what should we do?" the helmsman asked.

"Shut up and let me think a second," Edmonton yelled. *Who's closest to the forward hold?* Some of his men had gone ashore with the passengers and most of the rest were on the main deck supervising the loading of the launches. Engineering. *Hell, I left the chief engineer on the phone.*

The captain dashed to the intercom phone and snatched it up. "Johnson, are you still there?"

"Yes, sir. What's going on up there?"

"We're under attack."

"What?"

"Never mind why, we don't know and don't have time to talk. Now listen closely. Take your crew and any other men you see down there to the forward hold and open the crates that we picked up at our stop in China. Unpack the rifles and cartridges in them and bring them up as soon as you can."

"We're carrying firearms on board?"

"Damn it, I don't want to debate the issue. Just get the guns and ammo. We're going to be overrun and hijacked if you don't hurry, man."

"Aye, Captain."

The phone clattered in the captain's ear as the engineer on the other end of the line dropped the receiver onto the console. Edmonton looked back toward port and was horrified to see the machine gun swivel toward the bridge of his ship.

"Send an SOS," the captain ordered his radioman. "Tell them we're under attack and give the time and our position. Keep repeating the message until I tell you to stop or you're forcibly removed from your post."

"Aye, Captain," the pale sailor replied.

12

"I joined the Coast Guard to guard the coast," Seaman Shane Garwood grumbled as he held the rail of the pitching Coast Guard cutter.

"Don't you ever get tired of griping?" Petty Officer John Morris asked with a grin. "We were the farthest cutter from base and the closest to the SOS signal that just came in, so we go investigate. It's as simple as that."

The 220-foot vessel the two served aboard sported a five-inch cannon and two .50-caliber Browning machine guns. A heliport, minus the helicopter that sometimes rode aboard the boat, sat on its aft deck behind the two sailors who stood at the railing of the mast. From this position, they would later watch for any sign of the ship sending the SOS when they reached its coordinates.

"Well I don't like it when we get this far from land," Garwood finally said, hanging onto the rail as the cutter hit a high wave, causing the craft to list far to the port before righting itself. "I can always remember how to get back to where I started from on land. In the open sea there're no reference points. It gets to me."

"What has me spooked is the SOS," Morris said. "I heard they radioed that they were under attack."

"Pirates on the high seas," Garwood said melodramatically. "Hoist the Jolly Roger and steal some ship full of old people out to see all the tourist traps of the world."

"Laugh all you want," Morris said. "But a captain of a ship as big as the *Pleasure Run* isn't going to send out a weird SOS to better his career."

"Yeah, I suppose that's right. So what *do* you think's going on?"

Morris shook his head and pointed toward the forward deck. "One thing's for sure. If our captain's ordered our gunners to get the five-inch ready, he's expecting to hunt bears. This could be real serious."

Garwood unconsciously felt the automatic pistol holstered on his belt and looked morosely at the sea ahead of them, wishing that land were within swimming distance. He hated it when the ocean completely surrounded them and he couldn't get his bearings.

The machine gun raked the bridge of the *Pleasure Run,* strewing glass across the deck. That was a hell of a warning shot, Captain Edmonton thought as he scrambled toward the helmsman, who had sustained a bloody gash on his forehead.

"I'm all right, Captain," the crewman said. "Better check on Zellerman."

Edmonton turned toward where the helmsman nodded. Staying low, he crossed to the navigator.

One look at the lifeless eyes was all the captain needed; it was obvious the crewman was dead. For a moment he found his throat so tight he couldn't breathe. Then he gasped and looked away from his good friend's body.

The port hatch opened and a wide-eyed sailor entered the bridge. "Captain, I think you should hear this. The boat that just fired at us is hailing us—hollering up at us."

"Keep sending that SOS," Edmonton ordered the radioman. Then he turned toward the sailor who had entered the bridge. "Lead the way."

The two men scampered along the deck, past a string of screaming passengers who dashed toward the hatches leading to their quarters. The captain wondered when the strangers in the boat below would open fire again. "What do they sound like?" the captain asked.

"Weird," the sailor answered. "Foreign accent—Japanese, I think. Listen! They're starting again."

"American spies," the thickly accented voice called from below. "You surrender now or we will destroy your ship." Another blast racked the bridge, throwing slivers of glass across the deck.

There was a deathly silence as the ship rocked upward on a wave. Edmonton opened his eyes as the voice called from below. "We speak to captain now."

Where are those rifles? Edmonton fumed as he debated what to do next.

"Shit!" Johnson yelled, cracking open another of the crates. "Where the hell is the ammunition for these things!" So far the engineer and his two helpers had smashed eight of the crates open and found rifles and rocket launchers—but no ammunition for the Kalashnikov rifles. The crates all had fake stock numbers and labels, making it impossible to determine what was actually in any of them without first opening the wooden boxes.

"Couldn't we use one of these rockets?" Cox asked.

"Either of you know how to fire one of 'em?" Johnson asked, slapping a pry bar into the edge of another wooden box.

"No," Cox answered.

"Me neither," Johnson grunted, levering the bar downward. The lid of the crate split open to reveal more rifles. The engineer swore under his breath and looked around the storage compartment, trying to see some pattern to how the crates were arranged. "You fire a rocket wrong, and you're apt to crisp everything behind you or have the warhead drop in your lap."

"They're shooting that machine gun again!" Fernandez cried.

Johnson kicked the crate in frustration. "There must be some order to the way everything was stored in here. Cox, you look in that bunch of boxes over there. Fernandez, you check those at that end. That ammunition's got to be here somewhere."

A sailor came running to the hatch and hollered into the compartment. "Engineer Johnson, captain wants to know if you've got the rifles ready yet. He needs them on the double."

"We can't find the ammunition for them, Hopkins," Johnson explained to the deck hand. "And these rifles are so full of grease I'm not sure they'd be safe to fire without cleaning anyway. Tell the captain we're going as fast as we can."

"Any idea how long?"

"Damned if I know," Johnson said in frustration, yanking open a lid to discover a box of rockets. "None of the crates are labeled, so it's hit and miss. We might find the ammunition next box or it might be the first of never. Look at all the crates we've got left to open," he said, gesturing toward the stack with his pry bar.

"All right, I'll tell the captain." Hopkins turned away and ran down the passageway.

The three men continued to ransack the storage compartment until Cox finally yelled, "Here it is! Are these the right cartridges for the rifles?"

Johnson raced over, snatched one of the shiny brass cartridges from its box, and inserted it into an empty magazine. "Sure looks like it," he answered. "Fernandez, go tell the captain we found the ammunition for the rifles. We'll get a bunch loaded and bring them up."

The crewman raced down the hallway as Johnson showed Cox how to load the magazines for the Chinese rifles.

"We give you one minute and then we open fire and board you, killing all we see," the Japanese soldier warned from the small boat below Captain Edmonton.

The captain turned toward the messenger he had sent to check Johnson's progress. "Have they found the guns?"

The breathless sailor panted as he answered. "They have the guns—but not the ammunition. Johnson says none of the boxes are labeled and—"

"I get the picture," the captain said.

"Thirty seconds," the Japanese soldier called. "We will kill you if you don't surrender."

With the boiler tubes half dismantled, there was no way to start the engines in time to escape. And Edmonton didn't want to leave some of his crew and most of the passengers behind to the mercies of these madmen anyway. He had little choice.

"Take a message to Johnson," the captain told Hopkins before the officer stood to speak to the soldiers below. "Tell him to take the guns and ammunition and hide in the ship. You hide with him. Maybe you four will be able to help us later on. Good luck. Hurry."

As Hopkins dashed back toward the hatchway, Captain Edmonton stood and peered over the edge of the railing; he found himself looking down the coned barrel of a Type 1 heavy machine gun. "I'm the captain," he called to the soldiers below.

Johnson glanced up to see Hopkins sprinting through the hatchway. "Tell the captain we found the ammo," the engineer informed the breathless messenger.

"Captain says for you guys to get a bunch of

guns and ammunition and hide in the ship," Hopkins rapidly apprised the three sailors from engineering.

"What?" Johnson asked in disbelief.

"It looks like he's turning the ship over to the bastards who've been firing at us."

"That can't be," Cox said.

"Yeah," Fernandez agreed. "The captain would never give up our ship."

"He has to," Hopkins replied. "Those madmen were threatening to slaughter everyone on board— they've already killed a bunch of the passengers on shore and I heard Zellerman was killed by the volley that hit the bridge. I'm supposed to help you get some weapons and hide in the ship. We don't have much time. They're probably boarding us now."

Johnson swore, running his hand through his short black hair as he stood up, tossing the pry bar against the deck. "Okay, let's get busy. Hopkins, you get that crate of rockets over there. Drag it by the rope handle—it's too heavy to lift." The engineer looked around the storage compartment. "Cox, you and Fernandez grab that crate of ammo. I can carry four rifles—that's all we'll need, so there's no sense in taking more of them."

Within seconds the three sailors had followed the black engineer's orders and waited for him to lead the way.

Where to go, Johnson thought, inspecting the three sailors. Where was the best place for them to hide?

He finally came to a decision. "Follow me."

* * *

"We killed thirty-two of them," Lieutenant Ishimoto reported to his superior officer as the two men paced the deck of the *Pleasure Run*. "And our men captured nearly five hundred, some of whom are wounded. I'm ferrying soldiers here as fast as I can and sending our prisoners ashore. We suspect a few more passengers may be hidden below decks aboard this vessel."

"No doubt," Major Tashida said. "As big as it is, it will be hard to find anyone who wishes to remain hidden. Any armament?"

"We found these," the lieutenant answered, directing a soldier to bring a heavy plastic tube forward. "The picture instructions on the side here show how to operate it and look as if this machine is a rocket launcher. But it is hard to say without testing one."

"Select a detail and test-fire one at once," the major ordered. "Go to the far end of this ship and launch this thing toward the open sea. Such a weapon could be invaluable, as low as we are on stores of ammunition."

"We also found these rifles," Ishimoto said. "They fire these fat cartridges that are unlike any I've ever seen."

"What's this long appendage?" the major asked. "That isn't a magazine, is it?"

"Yes." Ishimoto nodded. "A detachable magazine. Each holds thirty cartridges and the guns seem to be gas operated."

Tashida studied the weapon held out by his

officer for his inspection. The amount of firepower such a weapon put out would be impressive. But it would also use cartridges at a tremendous rate in the hands of unskilled fighters. And there didn't even seem to be a bayonet on it. How like the Americans to create a weapon that killed from afar rather than using the cold steel of a blade.

"We have found no other weapons but this vessel is huge—like a small village inside. All types of clothing . . . clocks with tiny lights built into them. There are things here that are hard even to imagine."

"Are you familiar with the Greek myth of the Trojan horse?" Tashida asked, gazing over the brass railing toward his island.

"No, Major."

"In it, the Greek army fails to take the city of Troy because of its high walls. The Greek soldiers bring a giant wooden horse to the gates of the city and then the Greek warships sail away. The Trojans think their enemies have given up trying to take the city, and the Trojans drag the wooden horse into the center of their city and celebrate.

"But when those in the city fall asleep," Tashida continued, "a handful of Greek soldiers hidden in the hollow horse come out and open the gates, letting the Greeks, who have returned during the night, into the city to pillage and burn it." The major was silent for a moment.

"And you fear this ship may be the Americans' Trojan horse," Ishimoto said. "A way of getting us to lower our defenses and, somehow, to give them a toehold on our island."

Tashida looked the officer in the eye for a few

moments, nodding with the ghost of a smile on his face, happy the old lieutenant grasped his meaning so quickly.

"I will not bring too many of our men aboard, and we must be careful to post extra lookouts at the other side of the island."

"That is right. In the meantime, search the ship carefully for things we may use. But we must not celebrate this easy victory until we learn why the ship is here and what else the Americans may try. We must not let down our guard."

"We will be vigilant."

"Now I must return to the island to interrogate the prisoners. I will handle the defenses around the island myself, so you can concentrate on searching this ship."

The lieutenant and the other soldiers bowed as the old major left the deck of the American vessel.

13

Oz blinked at the bright sunlight streaming into his room, trying to recall where he was. Officers' quarters at Guam, he finally remembered. The racket that had awakened him started again. The furious pounding at the door continued and then stopped as quickly as it had begun. "Captain Carson, are you in there?" a muffled voice called from the hallway.

The airman rose with an oath, yanked his pants on, and crossed the room. "What?" he asked, jerking the door open.

"Sorry, sir." The private saluted. "I know you asked not to be disturbed, but we have an urgent message that has just been decoded. I was told to get it to you at once."

"Let's see it."

The messenger handed a sealed envelope to the officer who took it and quickly tore it open.

"I'm to wait in case you have any messages or a reply," the private said.

"Hang on just a minute then." Oz read rapidly, rubbing the stubble on his jaw. Then he looked up from the paper and spoke. "I want you to get all the helicopter teams rounded up for a meeting at . . . " The airman checked his watch. "At eleven hundred hours. Where's a secure room we could meet in?"

"The administration building has several conference rooms. Room number fifteen is usually open."

"Reserve it for us, and tell the teams we'll meet there at eleven hundred hours. I'll contact our ground crews myself. This message says Army Delta Forces are on the way. Any information about their ETA?"

"No, sir. The base commander received word that they just left the U.S. so it should be about twelve hours at least."

"Okay. Looks like we're all going to be staying here a little longer than expected."

"Yes, sir," the private replied as Oz returned his salute and closed the door. *Just one thing after another,* the pilot thought, hurriedly getting dressed. *But I guess that's what we get paid to do.*

Sergeant Marvin eyed the army work crews that had nearly disassembled and prepared for transport each of the four MH-60K helicopters that had flown onto the base the night before. Behind the crews, a giant Lockheed C-5A "Galaxy" cargo plane awaited the insertion of the choppers through its rear hatch. The plane was almost 68 meters wide and over 75 meters long. Its upward-hinging nose was down since it already contained the two Apache aircraft that had been stowed in it the day before. Once the four MH-60Ks were packed into the back of the C-5A transport, all six helicopters would start the long flight back to Fort Bragg.

The sergeant carefully supervised the loading team that had been working nearly forty-five minutes in the hot sun preparing Oz's helicopter for shipment; the brawny mechanic was known for his abilities to repair helicopters and had spent over a decade repairing, disassembling, and reassembling army aircraft of various types.

"All right," Marvin told his crew, which included of several new and very green men. "Now that the chopper's cleaned inside and out what do we do next, Cooper?"

"Uh . . . " the crewman said, rolling his eyes upward as he searched his mind. "Next we secure the loose equipment inside the helicopter so it can't slide around and damage anything."

"Exactly right," Marvin nodded. "Give the young man a cookie and let's get to work. And don't anybody dawdle—keep moving so we can get out of this sun. It's only going to get hotter."

"Sergeant Marvin," a familiar voice called from behind.

The mechanic turned from his crew, grinned, and saluted. "Captain Carson."

Oz returned the salute. "Afraid I've got some bad news for you. I just got word that we need to be on standby here. Something's up, and we may need to take all six of our choppers out at once."

One of the new men in Marvin's crew groaned, and the sergeant turned and glared at him before turning back to Oz. "So we need to reassemble these four copters plus the two Apaches?"

"I'm afraid that's right," the airman answered.

"Armament?"

"Better. Details are sketchy but it looks like there could be a hostage situation. I should know more in a while—the navy sent a Coast Guard cutter out to check on the situation."

"We'll get onto reassembling the choppers immediately," Marvin said, wiping his sweaty face with a rag. "I'll inform the other crews for you."

"Thanks. I'll get back to you if I find out anything else. This may be a wild goose chase, but we have to be ready just the same."

"Right, sir." Marvin saluted again as the airman turned to leave. The sergeant shook his head and then took a deep breath. "Okay you grease monkeys, listen up." The mechanic continued to explain the change in plans, raising his voice so he could be heard over the distant jet that screeched off the runway and wheeled out toward the ocean. As the sergeant proceeded, the faces of the soldiers in front of him fell as they realized they were going to have to undo all the packing they'd labored so hard to accomplish.

Petty Officer Morris stood on the bridge of U.S. Coast Guard cutter number 624 as the ship came to quarter speed, bobbing up and down on the indigo waves. Ahead of them sat the *Pleasure Run*, the vessel that had sent out a frantic SOS, but which now could not be raised on the radio.

"Captain, that island is on the charts," the navi-

gator said, bringing a map over for the commanding officer to see.

"Doesn't make any difference now," Captain
Querner replied, giving the chart only a casual
glance. "Although I guess it is nice to know we
haven't discovered someplace that's completely
unknown." He turned. "Mr. Morris."

"Yes, Captain," the petty officer answered.

"Go down to the deck and tell the men to stay
sharp. I don't see a living soul on that ship. It looks
like something's very wrong, so have them lock
and load their rifles. But do not fire unless I give
the command. I don't want any accidents."

"Aye, Captain," Morris said, saluting sharply
and then turning to leave the bridge. He climbed
down to the main deck and quickly joined the men
standing around the breakwater ahead of the five-
inch cannon. The men wore steel pot helmets and
combination flotation and flak jackets.

"Captain says to lock and load," the petty officer told them. "But do not fire unless ordered to.
Everyone got that?"

Several of the sailors nodded; the others
seemed in a daze.

"So no shooting without orders," he added,
hoping to hammer the message into everyone's
brain.

Each sailor carefully shoved a magazine into his
Steyr AUG rifle, pushed the square safety to its safe
position in the pistol grip, then jacked back the
bolt and released it so it clattered forward, chambering a shell in the barrel of the bullpup firearm.

"Spread out," Morris ordered the men after they

had loaded their rifles. "Stay down behind the fore-castle and keep clear of our five-incher. I don't want to be cleaning your brains off the deck because you forgot to duck when the cannon opened up."

Once the petty officer was satisfied the fifteen sailors weren't bunching up and were clear of the cannon, he turned to the gun crew. "Be ready to fire; there's no telling what we're getting into out here."

Morris paused and glared at the gunner, who was elbowing his partner. "This isn't some Sunday picnic, sailor. The captain is dead serious and you should be, too. The SOS from that ship mentioned armed troops; we might very well be facing a supe-rior force."

"Yes, sir," the chastened gunner responded, wiping the grin off his face.

"Remember, do not fire unless ordered to," Morris repeated to all the men at the front of the vessel before turning and quickly jogging along the deck to the aft end of the boat.

He passed the helideck, which stood empty, went on back to the quarterdeck, and repeated his instructions to the sailors back there. Satisfied all the men on deck were ready, he returned forward to stand beside his friend, Seaman Garwood, who headed the main boarding team.

The sailor perused the cruise ship they were bearing down on. "The deck of the *Pleasure Run* appears to be empty," he muttered as Morris took up a position beside him. "Damned weird if you ask me. But at least we're finally close to land."

"And the captain found the island on the charts. Everyone was real spooked on the bridge when they thought we'd found an uncharted island. Guess it's just a chunk of real estate that's too out of the way for anyone to take much notice of."

"Well, it's a chunk of real estate I'm noticing," Garwood said. "Is the captain going to take us right up to that ship?"

"I don't know how else we can find out what's going on," Morris said as the ship continued forward at quarter speed, slowly crossing the remaining distance to the *Pleasure Run*. "I imagine we'll be boarding it, so you'd better have your team ready."

"Those are bullet holes along their bridge," the sailor next to Garwood muttered.

Miller noticed that the row of sailors all raised their rifles when they saw that the ship had indeed been fired on. Good, the petty officer thought. Maybe they'll all take this more seriously now.

The bullhorn above the bridge came on, and most of the sailors on the foredeck covered one or both ears, knowing from the hiss that the volume was turned up to its highest setting.

"Attention, *Pleasure Run*," the captain's voice boomed metallically from the speaker. "This is the U.S. Coast Guard. Is anyone aboard?"

There was no reply.

"*Pleasure Run*, we have received your SOS and request permission to board you. I repeat, this is the U.S. Coast Guard."

There was still no answer, no sign of life on the derelict ship.

The volume of the loudspeaker went lower as the captain spoke to those on the deck in front of him. "Mr. Morris, secure us to the ship and then prepare the ladder and the boarding detail to go aboard the vessel with you."

"Aye, Captain," Morris hollered toward the bridge and then faced the sailors along the deck. "Ready with the lines," he called. "You four get the boarding ladder ready. Garwood, you and your team will accompany me onto the ship."

"Yes, sir," Garwood said, his face a mask.

The Coast Guard cruiser sliced through the warm ocean, turning to head for the low aft deck of the *Pleasure Run,* slowing to a near stop while the helmsman jockeyed them as close as was safe.

"Cast lines," Morris ordered.

Two sailors tossed grappling hooks across the space between the two vessels; the metal hooks clattered over the brass railing of the *Pleasure Run*'s deck, catching as the sailors jerked them taut. Then the other crewmen activated the winches connected to the lines, slowly pulling the cutter toward the leisure craft that dwarfed the smaller Coast Guard boat.

"Secure the lines," Morris ordered. Rather than watch the sailors, his attention was drawn to the ship that now towered above their railing, making him aware of how exposed the cutter's deck was to anyone who might be above them.

"Attention, *Pleasure Run,*" the captain's voice boomed over the speaker again. "We are boarding you now. This is the U.S. Coast Guard."

"Great, nothing like warning everybody up there so they can catch us on the ladders," one of the crewmen muttered.

"Stow it, sailor," Morris ordered. "Get that ladder up there on the double."

The four sailors manning the light ladder carefully raised it to the deck of the ship above.

Petty Officer Morris swallowed and then climbed onto the bucking ladder. "Gentlemen, if you'll follow me."

"Yes, sir," Garwood said, trying to smile as he sidled up to the ladder and waited for the officer to get far enough up it so he could follow.

Within moments Morris, Garwood, and the squad Garwood headed were on the deck of the *Pleasure Run*.

"Look at all the junk on the deck," Garwood whispered, eyeing the hats, articles of clothing, and deck chairs scattered across the surface of the ship in front of them. "Looks like they left in a hurry."

"You don't suppose there's a boiler about to explode or something dangerous, sir?" one of the nervous sailors asked.

"The SOS didn't mention that," the petty officer answered. "They said they were under attack. So stay sharp. You two stay here on the fantail. The rest of us will go on up and check out the bridge. Maybe we can find out something up there."

Lieutenant Ishimoto turned to Private Kuroshima. "Did you understand what they said?"

"Most of it," the translator replied. "They said they are the U.S. Coast Guard and are getting ready to board the ship."

"Since they've already boarded the ship, your news comes a little late," Ishimoto said. "Stay close to me so I can know *instantly* what they are saying."

"Yes, sir."

"Their helmets and rifles look strange," the officer said, peeping over the rim of the bridge at the men below. "They have changed their uniforms since I last saw pictures of them—or perhaps this is a special branch of sailors."

"Their officer doesn't carry a sword, and their short rifles have no bayonets," Kuroshima whispered. "Hardly the weapons of a true warrior."

Ishimoto said nothing. Sometimes he thought the Japanese emphasized the power of the blade over the bullet too much. Bullets killed just as effectively as a blade and had the added dimension of operating over long distances. But the old man said nothing, knowing that to do so would contradict much of what Major Yashida had hammered into his troops over the years they had occupied the island.

The officer turned toward the riflemen around him. "They didn't see the men hidden along the main deck and are coming this way. Get ready."

Johnson stood in the darkness, a loaded Kalashnikov held tightly in his hand.

"We've got to do something," Cox whispered to him. "If we let the Coast Guard just sit out there, the Japanese soldiers are going to slaughter them all."

"No way, man," Fernandez argued. "We're dead if we make a peep. They'll find us for sure."

"Shhh," Johnson hissed. "Be quiet and stay right here. I think I might be able to warn them without giving us away."

He turned toward the three sailors. "If I succeed, all hell's going to break loose. So I'll be coming back here in a hurry. If no one's on my tail, I'll knock three times and you let me in, pronto. If I don't come back, you guys are on your own."

The three watched silently as Johnson cracked the hatchway open and peered into the darkened hallway. The engineer clicked the safety off his rifle and stepped out. "See you later," he told them and then closed the hatch.

14

"Fire!" Lieutenant Ishimoto commanded.

His riflemen rose with the new automatic rifles they'd discovered on the ship and fired from the bridge toward the men on the deck, most of whom fell immediately under the withering volley, with only one sailor escaping into the ship.

"Cease fire," Ishimoto cried to those on the bridge. He studied the line of soldiers who had been hidden along the rail. Ordered to attack after his men on the bridge fired, those below him now leaned over the railing and shot at the Americans on the cutter below.

Ishimoto turned to the soldiers standing around him. "Hurry down there and reinforce our men. With any luck we may be able to kill the crewmen on the cutter before they can counterattack."

Captain Querner stood frozen at the intense fire coming over the railing from the ship above him. Most of his men had fallen in the first wave of fire. Finally he willed himself to move, clicking on the microphone in his hands. "Return fire!" he cried to the few left on the deck. "Get us out of here," he ordered the helmsman.

"Captain, we're still moored to the ship," the helmsman cried over the pounding fire of the five-inch cannon on the deck. The shell smashed through the hull of the *Pleasure Run,* exploding below decks with a muffled detonation.

"Full power—we'll break away so we can put some distance between us," the captain cried, ducking as a volley from above pocked the front port, sending a sprinkling of white dust into the bridge as the bulletproof glass caught and held the projectiles.

The helmsman raised an eyebrow as he relayed the message to the engine room. The boat started to strain at the lines but failed to break free. "We're stuck here, Captain," the helmsman reported, yelling over the booming of the five-inch gun on deck.

Querner said nothing, his eyes riveted to the Japanese soldiers at the railing of the *Pleasure Run.* As he watched, they raised rocket launchers and fired them in unison.

The rocket engines exploded in bursts of light, sending a jet of flame behind the soldiers. The missiles streaked toward the Coast Guard cutter, one landing harmlessly on the empty deck, erupting in a blaze of fire. The second struck the cannon, instantly killing the two sailors who manned it, even though little damage was done to the gun itself.

The third came directly toward the bridge, crashing into the glass and exploding on its surface, instantly killing all those inside with the shards of tempered glass that slashed through the compartment, cutting the crewmen to ribbons.

Johnson crept up the dark stairwell inside the *Pleasure Run,* silently cursing because he hadn't been able to reach the deck or a porthole in time to fire warning shots to alert the Coast Guard. He tried to walk quietly along the metal steps to reach an upper deck, hoping to throw in his lot with the other Americans and perhaps defeat the men holding the ship.

Inching forward, his eyes strained to see in the blackness. Explosions again rocked the outside of the ship. They're really going at it, he thought. Would the Coast Guard prevail?

Visually sweeping the stairs ahead of him, Johnson spotted a shape in the darkness, cautiously moving downward toward him. The engineer flattened himself against the bulkhead, raising his Kalashnikov but not wanting to fire unless he had to, for fear of attracting unwanted attention.

The figure coming down didn't seem to be armed.

Johnson debated what to do as the man came on, oblivious of the sailor's presence. "Hold it right there, buddy," Johnson said, wondering if the Japanese soldier could understand him.

"All right," Morris said, raising his hands.

"Who are you?" Johnson asked.

"U.S. Coast Guard," the man answered. "Petty Officer Morris."

"No shit? What's going on out there, Morris?"

"They're slaughtering us, near as I can tell. All my men were killed on the deck when we headed for the bridge. Now they're firing at the cutter with rockets. With our boat moored to this ship, the captain couldn't pull out of range."

Johnson said nothing but recalled how the Japanese soldiers had been test-firing the rockets they'd found shortly before the Coast Guard had arrived. *We should have set the hold on fire and destroyed the weapons,* the engineer thought. But there hadn't been time, and they hadn't had the opportunity to think things through.

"Come on," Johnson ordered. "Let's get out of here. Are you hurt?"

"Just ripped my flak jacket when I dived through a hatch."

"Follow me. Watch your step and stay close." Johnson turned and retraced his path. If the Coast Guard was getting wiped out, there was nothing he or Morris could do to help them now. At least he could take this sailor back to the hideout they'd improvised behind the engine room.

They reached the bottom of the stairs and Johnson paused, hearing footsteps echoing in the dimly lit corridor ahead of him. The engineer raised his rifle, squinting in the darkness. *Are they Japanese or some of our guys?* Johnson wondered, unsure what to do.

Then the two men ahead of him spoke.

Japanese, Johnson realized, mashing the trigger of his rifle and hanging on to the weapon as it rattled a long burst of automatic fire. The blast echoed through the stairwell, deafening the engineer. In the muzzle flash, he saw the two soldiers hit by several of the bullets that cracked down the narrow passageway and ricocheted off the metal bulkhead.

Both the Japanese soldiers dropped.

"Come on," Johnson yelled to Morris. "They'll be all over us now if we stay here."

The engineer leapt over the fallen soldiers on the deck and turned to see Morris pick up one of the new automatic rifles the two had been carrying. Johnson turned back and glanced down the passageway that intersected theirs. Observing no one, he raced to a second stairwell at the end of the corridor and went down it two steps at a time toward the double doors that led to the lower deck.

As Johnson shoved the doors open, he spotted a Japanese soldier with an old bolt-action rifle; the trooper jumped forward, firing his weapon as he came. The muzzle flash blazed in the dim light; the bullet cracked past the engineer's bald head, and the smoke stung his eyes and nose, making it impossible for him to see.

The soldier worked the action of his rifle, quickly chambering another round.

Morris pushed past Johnson, shouldering his rifle and triggering it in a blur of motion. The hail of bullets from the weapon slashed into the Japanese soldier's face, splattering the passageway with blood. The nearly headless man fell backward into the corridor, his rifle dropping beside his ragged body.

"Thanks," Johnson said, stepping over the fallen soldier and nearly losing his footing in the brass cartridges that rolled along the slick deck. The engineer fought off the urge to vomit and hurried down the passageway, listening to the hammering of boots on the deck above.

The Japanese must be searching the ship again, he thought. He turned and jogged down another corridor.

The young sailor behind Johnson fired his rifle.

The engineer spun around to see two Japanese soldiers beyond Morris drop to the deck. Another explosion outside the ship rocked the air with its fury.

"Come on, we're almost there," Johnson told the sailor behind him. The two turned down another passageway, passing the engine room. The engineer came to a stop and rapidly opened a hatchway that seemed to lead into a dead end room filled with trash.

"Close the hatch after us," Johnson instructed the sailor. The engineer entered the room and pulled back a plastic tarp covered with refuse, revealing another small hatch that had been hidden in back of it. Johnson banged on the metal door three times with the buttstock of his rifle and then waited.

The hatch cracked open. "That you, Johnson?"

"No, it's Santa Claus. Get back so we can come in. I've brought some company."

Johnson let the Coast Guard officer pass him and then carefully pulled the tarp over the opening and closed the hatch behind them.

"Well, Morris, you might as well sit down and relax," Johnson said, turning to the new addition to their party. "We're going to have to make some plans to figure out how to get out of this mess."

"All the American sailors save one on the cutter are dead," the soldier said.

"A prisoner?" Ishimoto asked.

"Yes, knocked unconscious by our first volley. Someone also seems to be below decks. We can't tell if it is one of the original passengers or one of the Coast Guard contingent that came aboard. Five of our men were found dead below deck."

"We'll continue to search the ship then," Ishimoto said. "How many other casualties?"

"Two dead, six wounded. The Americans didn't have time to use their weapons effectively."

"Transfer as much ordnance from the cutter to shore as you can and then scuttle the Coast Guard vessel—we have no use for a boat that large in the island defenses. Take the prisoner ashore, too."

"*Hai*," the soldier said, sharply saluting the old lieutenant and then turning to leave.

The U.S. Air Force F-22 streaked high above Kakira, the rumble of its jet engines inaudible to those on the ground because of the altitude at which the stealth fighter flew. Scrambled from Guam moments after contact had been lost with the Coast Guard cutter, the black composite aircraft now flew like a bat-shaped shadow, unnoticed by those it spied on from two thousand feet.

The pilot overshot the island, turned off his cameras, and switched on his radio. "My first photo pass is complete," he reported. "I'm not getting any radar or radio signals from the ground," he added after checking the screen connected to the "Spy Pack" he carried in his bomb bay. "Shall I make another pass? Over."

"That's a roger," ground control responded. "Our guys want to know what the hell's going on out there. Then head back so we can see what you've got. Over and out."

The pilot pushed his stick to the side, bringing the jet around for another pass of Kakira. As he neared the island, he thumbed on the automatic cameras mounted to the stealth jet. Within six seconds the second pass was completed and the pilot aligned his F-22 onto a course that would take him back to Andersen Air Force Base on Guam.

15

The Night Stalkers and one marine lieutenant sat in metal folding chairs in an air-conditioned room that felt cold enough to be in the Arctic circle rather than on Guam. The sixteen soldiers listened intently as Oz described their upcoming mission that would commence at nightfall.

The pilot stood behind a small walnut lectern. Behind him was a map of Kakira, which had been created by air force personnel working from old charts they had located on the base.

Because of the possibility that hostages were involved, and the nearest U.S. Navy task force was five days away from Kakira, it was impossible for the U.S. government simply to land a large amphibious force to sweep the island, backing the troops up with the massive air power a carrier could offer. Instead, it had been decided that the Night Stalkers would ferry a platoon of U.S. Marines, led by Lieutenant Vasco, onto the island where the troopers would obtain any information they could about the enemy and engage in "body snatching"—taking prisoners for interrogation.

Through these efforts, it was hoped the American leaders could assess the dangers and the strengths of any terrorist forces holding the island. The missions involved in rescuing the hostages had been designated as part of Operation Avenging Storm, whose ultimate goal was the rescue of the Americans being held on Kakira.

The marine contingent would withdraw after only a brief stay on the island, and information they garnered would be evaluated by the CIA and military intelligence before any major rescue attempt was launched. In addition to ferrying the marines to the island and taking them back to Guam, the Night Stalkers would also offer light air support if it was called for on the intelligence-gathering mission.

"So that's about it," Oz told the soldiers after briefing them on their assignment.

"What about those air reconnaissance photos you mentioned?" Marine Lieutenant Vasco asked, tapping the end of a new cigarette on the chair in front of him.

"The air force promised the photos would be here," Oz answered, pacing to one side of the lectern. "But they seem to be overdue," he added, checking his watch.

"Speak of the devil," O.T. said as the rear door of the room snapped open and Air Force Ensign Addis entered.

"Sorry to keep you waiting, gentlemen," the officer said as he approached the front of the room and saluted Oz. "One of our people spotted something in the photos we took of Kakira. The details looked—and are—important. And they have some very odd ramifications for your mission."

"We're all ears," Oz said, glancing around the room at his fellow servicemen. "Let's see what you've got."

"All right," the air force officer said, pulling at his tie. "I'm going to pass out some packets of photos that we took just a half hour ago. Ink's practically still wet on them. I think you'll find them very interesting."

He stepped among the army airmen and the marine and quickly distributed the packets of photos, then returned to the lectern with one copy of his own. "You'll note that the photos inside each envelope are numbered in the upper right corner," he continued, opening his own packet.

The ensign tapped the edge of the stack against the lectern to straighten them and then placed the photos in front of him. "We'll start with print number one—that's how the air force usually starts, and I'll assume the army and marines do likewise," he added with a grin.

"On photo one," he continued, "you'll notice that we have two vessels in the small cove on the southwest corner of the island. The larger is definitely a commercial liner and the smaller is a U.S. Coast Guard cutter. The dark smudges around the cutter—you can barely see them in this photo—appear to be small boats, possibly the launches from the passenger ship."

"Those are the two vessels that have been lost," Marine Lieutenant Vasco suggested.

"Air force intelligence is not Machiavellian

enough to think these are anything other than the *Pleasure Run* and the cutter," the ensign acknowledged, pulling a stick of gum from his pocket and unwrapping it. "There's not much to see here; if you'll turn to photo two."

He paused as the group shuffled their pictures to the next print. "This was taken on our jet's second pass of the island. Though it's impossible to tell from looking at these pictures, we took careful measurements using reference points on the land mass. We found that both ships are in the exact same positions on both passes. Neither moved, suggesting that both are anchored in the harbor.

"On to photo three," Addis said, turning to the next picture with the rest of the men in the room. "This is a computer enhancement of an enlargement of the cutter."

"Those are bodies lying on the cutter?" one of the airmen asked.

"Yes," Addis answered. "And the bodies are in the same positions during both passes, suggesting they're dead or unconscious. There are also men walking among them; they're carrying long rifles—longer than the bullpup rifles the crewmen carry. Extremely long barrels on these rifles by modern standards."

"What are the shadowy areas around the cannon?" Vasco asked. "Are those from clouds or actually on the deck?"

"Those look like burned patches," Oz submitted.

"That's right." Addis nodded. "The spots are on the deck, and we believe the blackened areas around the cannon and the bridge were created by explosive ordnance—they're consistent with the signature of shells or missile hits."

One of the airmen whistled.

Oz spoke. "So we are definitely against not only an armed contingent but one with pretty sophisticated weapons?"

"It would appear so." Ensign Addis nodded.

"Any damage on the *Pleasure Run?*" an airman asked.

"Nothing we could spot from the air. The decks of the *Pleasure Run* are completely empty. That in itself is odd for a luxury ship."

"So any idea where the passengers are?" the marine lieutenant asked.

"No hard evidence. But we're assuming that the passengers and crew are either below deck or—more likely—have been transported to the island."

Addis paused to see if there were any more questions and then continued. "Photo four is of the entire island. And this brings us to what held me up getting here. Those dark, weblike patterns are military emplacements."

"Military emplacements?" Vasco asked. "Who in the world has a military emplacement out in the middle of nowhere?"

"Officially no one," Addis said. "But that's not the half of it. One of our new hotshots who's made a hobby of studying old fortifications thinks the emplacements you're looking at resemble the classic Japanese formations used in World War II."

"Then these are just leftovers from the war?" O.T. asked.

"We thought of that," Addis answered. "But the

tropical storms that come through here would have erased those by now. The sands drift and erase such fortifications in just a matter of a few years. It appears someone is maintaining the system. Also, those trenches at the north end of the island—toward the top of the photo—are new, judging from the lack of vegetation around them. We estimate them to be less than a year old at the most. It's hard to see, but there are also several machine-gun nests along the trenches—these appear to be manned."

"Wait a minute," Vasco said. "You're telling us that someone's copying World War II vintage fortifications out in the middle of nowhere and now they've attacked two vessels?"

Addis rubbed his chin a moment before speaking. "Let's back up for a minute and look at the history of Kakira. Because the island had little strategic significance to the Allies during the war, it was simply leapfrogged by the Allied troops as they fought their way across the Pacific. It was assumed that the island wasn't occupied at that time, but no U.S. forces ever landed there to check. Our two nuclear bombs then brought an abrupt end to the hostilities when the Japanese surrendered."

"And after the war," Oz said, "with the advent of long-range jet aircraft, the island's strategic value dropped to zero, right?"

"Exactly," Addis agreed. "With no minerals or other useful materials on Kakira, no one was interested in even visiting it. And all shipping routes are far to the north of it; as far as anyone knew it was just a worthless desert island."

"Hold on," Vasco said. "Then you're saying that Japanese soldiers who never learned that World War II ended could still be holding the island?"

"That sounds pretty farfetched," one of the airmen ventured.

"I concede that," Ensign Addis nodded. "It's most unlikely. But you can't argue that those emplacements are new and well maintained. Somebody made them for some reason."

"And someone attacked the *Pleasure Run* and the cutter," Oz added. He tapped the photo. "*Something*'s going on there and that's where we come in."

"I have three squads of marines ready and waiting to find out what the hell is going on there," Lieutenant Vasco said, sitting erect in his chair, "World War II vintage Japanese soldiers or not."

"I might add that our reconnaissance plane detected no sign of radar or ground radio transmissions," Addis put in.

"So they might not detect us coming in or operating over the island," Death Song suggested. "And their abilities to communicate across the island might be limited as well."

"That's correct," the ensign agreed.

"If they're that low tech," Vasco said, rubbing his jaw, "then we might also have a distinct advantage with our night vision equipment when we go in tonight."

"I think we're getting a lot of 'mights' here," Oz said. "I think we'd better treat this group, whoever they are, as if they have modern equipment and then hope they don't."

"Yeah." Vasco nodded in agreement. "Ensign Addis, you've even got *me* halfway believing that there're World War II vintage soldiers on the island. You're right, Captain Carson. As the old saying goes, go in hot and hope they're not."

"I see your people have blown up a photo of the central section of the island," Oz said, turning back to Addis.

"Yes, we believe there's one section of the island that you might be able to land on without running into any resistance or booby traps."

"We're all ears," the army pilot said.

CHAPTER

16

Seaman Shane Garwood had regained consciousness after being trussed by the Japanese soldiers on the *Pleasure Run*. He thought he was a dead man when the volley from the bridge had caught his squad in the open on the deck. But the bullet that had knocked him unconscious had apparently glanced off his helmet, leaving him with a pounding headache, but alive.

Keep track of the route, he ordered himself as his ragged captors herded him and the last of the passengers from the *Pleasure Run* into small launches piled high with booty taken from the ship. The group of prisoners was transferred to land and quickly led up the beach, plodding along awkwardly in the cords that bound them, the soldiers gibbering at the captives every step of the way.

"These guys speaking Japanese or what?" Garwood asked the thin tourist herded beside him, but the point of a bayonet being jabbed into his back warned him not to speak.

The sailor glanced toward the eight other prisoners with him: three women and five men, all trussed with crude cordage just as he was. The drab uniforms of the two soldiers who guarded them were in sharp contrast to the garish clothing of the passengers from the ship.

The uniforms of the soldiers were as crude as the cordage that bound the prisoners and it, too, appeared to be homemade, coarsely woven and pieced together. The uniforms seemed vaguely familiar to Garwood. He racked his brain for a moment and then noticed the ancient rifles the soldiers carried. *They're dressed like something out of an old movie,* he told himself. *Japanese imperial soldiers. What was going on?*

The soldiers shoved the prisoners onto a pathway that led past a small dock, hidden from the air by a thatched roof and the palms around it. Garwood noted the boats moored at the rough-hewn plank dock. *That's something to remember for later,* he thought. The prisoners were shoved into the jungle growth until they entered a trench that led to a primitive tunnel, its roof supported by hewn palm logs. Garwood glanced at the sun one last time to get his bearings and then concentrated on memorizing the route ahead of him as he passed into the tunnel.

Inside the mouth of the narrow shaft the prisoners came to a stop while one of the guards took a torch from a niche in the sand and rock wall and then lit it, using an ember from a small bamboo tube he carried. The torch sputtered to life as he blew on it, crackling as the oil on the rag heated up. The soldier motioned that the prisoners should follow him, and the Americans quickly fell into line, conditioned by the bayonet pricks they had received coming up the beach.

The soldier led them through a rabbit's warren of underground passageways that twisted and turned at seemingly random points along the way, branching and intersecting at odd junctures. The torch he carried flickered as he walked, his shadow dancing along the walls like a bent gnome.

From time to time they passed large caverns cut into the earth. Some were storage rooms containing supplies, many with crates and boxes of rotting wood or rusty containers marked with Japanese characters. Occasionally they passed a room with bamboo screened walls and lamps, around which soldiers or even what appeared to be families sat eating, their conversation ceasing as they stared at the prisoners being led past.

Memory, don't fail me now, Garwood told himself, realizing that if he had a chance to escape, it would be essential to remember the way he'd entered the complex web of tunnels that seemed to honeycomb the island. Then he spotted the small markings cut into the wooden support beams. *Just like street signs,* he thought, noting the symbol that the soldier was following.

An underground city with street signs. *Maybe that blow on the head killed me and this is hell,* he thought. Maybe. But he'd still keep track of their path. He might be entering hell but he damned sure would try to leave it first chance he got.

Just keep track of the way out.

* * *

Captain Edmonton sat huddled in the darkness, his arms wrapped around his legs, his head resting on his knees.

"When will this stop?" one of the prisoners asked in the darkness.

Edmonton didn't answer because he didn't know. None of it made sense. The Japanese took them out one by one for questioning and, when they didn't get the answers they wanted, tortured the prisoner they had selected. The captain knew what they were doing; his throbbing hand now minus its fingernails attested to the facts. But why they were doing it or how long it would go on he didn't know.

"You are the captain of the ship?" the translator had asked Edmonton after dragging him out of his cell.

"Yes," he'd replied, straining the bonds that held him in the primitive wooden chair his captors had tied him to. "And I demand that you release my crew and passengers. We are American citizens, and our country is not at war with you or anyone else. You have no right to keep us."

The translator spoke to the officer standing next to him and then turned back to Edmonton. "You are prisoners of war and we can do with you as we please. Even though you are unworthy after surrendering your ship without a fight, Major Tashida will spare your life until we have killed all the others—which is what we will do if none of you tells us the truth."

"What secrets do you want to know?" Edmonton asked. "I have nothing to hide."

"Why did the United States military send you here, and when will they attack our island?"

"You're mad," Edmonton said. "The United States doesn't even know this place exists. But I can tell you one thing; they *will* be here when they find out what you've done."

"When?"

"Who knows?" Edmonton laughed. "Do you think I'm a mind reader or something?"

The translator turned to the major and told him what the captain had said. The officer nodded, then turned toward the table beside him and carefully selected one of the tools from the assortment of knives, picks, and saws. He brought the pliers over to Edmonton as the soldiers grabbed the captain's hand and held it against the arm of the chair.

The major had smiled as he fastened the jaws of the tool to Edmonton's fingernail.

Now the screams of the last woman the guards had dragged from their sandy cell echoed down the corridor outside, and Edmonton tried to close them from his mind but couldn't. How were they going to bring this to a stop?

One thing Edmonton knew: he was the captain of the *Pleasure Run* and that woman, even though he didn't know her name, was one of his passengers for whose safety he was responsible. The screaming stopped abruptly and was replaced by an ominous silence. The captain tried to make some sense of the situation, but the pain in his hand made it impossible to think clearly.

The rough door of the tiny room opened, and a flaring torch was thrust into the room, making Edmonton squint at its brightness. He steeled himself against the soldiers who would come in and yank out another of the six cowering Americans in the cell for questioning and torture.

Instead, nine more prisoners were herded into the cell and the door slammed behind them, again leaving the chamber in darkness.

"Welcome to hell," one of the prisoners told the newcomers.

Dan Brooks glanced up as the Japanese soldiers threw the sailor into his cell but felt no curiosity as to where the man had come from. Instead, he searched frantically for a pulse at his wife's neck and was startled by how cold she had become. In the brief torchlight, he had seen that her face was deathly pale.

He couldn't find her pulse. He placed his ear over her heart and heard nothing, felt no breathing. Though he failed to experience it emotionally, he knew she had bled to death in his arms while the Japanese soldiers refused to do anything other than shove and kick him whenever he pleaded for help. Little by little her blood had soaked into the sandy floor of the cell, and with it, her life had drained away.

"What kind of animals are these?" he muttered, rocking back and forth, still cradling his wife to his chest in the darkness of his cell. He listened to the screams of the woman the soldiers had dragged from the cell and now tortured.

When he'd been in the service, Dan had heard stories of the mistreatment of military prisoners and civilians. But that had been nearly a half century ago, he thought. The war was over. What was going on now? Why were these people here and why had they taken the ship over?

One thing was sure, he pledged in the darkness. He would kill whoever was responsible for his wife's death.

Johnson crept down the dark corridor, carefully feeling his way to save the batteries of his flashlight. "We're there," he whispered, his fingers snagging on the edge of the hatchway.

He slid his rifle across his back, the string he'd used as a sling cutting into his shoulder with the weight of the firearm. He carefully unlatched the metal hatch and swung it out of the way, producing a whining squeak that echoed in the corridor. *Bet they could hear that clear on the bridge,* he told himself. He stepped over the threshold and into the galley. "Stay here and keep a sharp lookout," he ordered Cox.

"Okay," the sailor whispered back.

Johnson carefully felt his way past the scarred butcher block table in the center of the room, nearly tripping in the darkness over a kettle that lay in the middle of the deck, and then felt his way along the greasy stove tops toward his goal.

He heard a sound outside in the hall and swung around, moving his head so fast he could see glowing spots. "Anybody out there?" he whispered. "Cox?"

"It's clear," the sailor answered. "Sorry about the noise."

I'm going to have a heart condition if we ever get out of this mess, Johnson told himself, listening to his heart pound in the darkness. He turned back and felt his way until he reached the storage closet built into the bulkhead of the ship.

He tried the latch. Locked. That was lucky, because he knew where the cook hid the key—he'd seen the man hide it once when he'd been in the galley to bum a cup of coffee. *But is the key still here?* Johnson wondered. He reached up to the rim of the hatch and felt along it until his fingers touched what he was searching for. He quickly grasped it, brought it down to the latch, and carefully felt in the darkness for the keyhole. He inserted the key and turned it until a loud snap announced that the door was open.

Johnson dropped the key into his pocket and then unfastened the hatch and pulled it open. Reaching behind himself, he extracted the flashlight from his hip pocket and flicked it on.

Not only are we going to eat, the engineer thought, a smile spreading across his face, *we're going to eat like fat cats.* His big problem would be deciding which cans of the gourmet food spread on the shelves in front of him would be the best ones to carry back to their hideout.

"Hey, Cox," Johnson called in a loud whisper. "Come here and help me. You like caviar?"

"Shhh," Cox hissed. "Someone's coming."

The engineer switched off his flashlight, transfering it to his left as he brought his rifle around from behind his back. Kneeling in the darkness, he placed the flashlight under the handguard of the rifle and pushed the safety into its fire position.

Major Tashida wiped the bloody *tanto* across the dead woman's blouse and then paused to study the wide-eyed stare that had frozen on her pale face. "That is enough for today," the major told the soldiers around him, replacing his knife in its sheath. "Private Kuroshima," he said to his translator, "we will begin again tomorrow, so come to my quarters at sunrise. In the meantime," he told the soldiers around him, "take this corpse back to the cell you brought her from and toss her in with the others. Nothing like sleeping in a room with a corpse to loosen a prisoner's tongue."

"*Hai,*" the soldiers said in unison before roughly gathering the mutilated body and dragging it down the tunnel.

The major turned from the entrance and stuck the *tanto* into his sash. *All of these spies tell the same lies,* he thought, eyeing the fingertip lying on the floor. He ground it under his sandal until it was covered with the sand of the floor.

Why did the Americans persist in this insanity and keep sending more people to him? One thing was sure, he had plenty more prisoners to question. Perhaps one of them would break and tell the truth before being sent to the land of the dead.

The major smirked at the thought of the work that needed to be done.

17

The Night Stalkers flight teams and the marine platoon filed through the night toward the six helicopters, which were positioned in a line on the tarmac at Andersen Air Force Base. A cool breeze from the ocean blew across the sand, driving away the small insects that flitted around the runway lights. In the distance a jet thundered as it took off; then the night was still, with only the soldiers' boots and the rattle of equipment breaking the calm.

Four of the Night Stalkers airmen headed for the McDonnell Douglas AH-64 Apache attack helicopters parked at either end of the line of aircraft; a gunner climbed into the front compartment of each while a pilot mounted the cabin behind him. Each Apache sported two stubby wings extending from its sides; the wings held eight laser-guided Hellfire missiles and two rocket pods. A 30-mm chain gun sat under the chin of each Apache, slaved to a control system mounted in the gunner's helmet. The weapon systems of each gunship were coupled with the aircraft's forward-looking infrared and "Longbow" radar systems, giving it the capability to engage targets in total darkness during all types of weather.

The four MH-60Ks between the Apaches were identical, with their weapons pods mounted to the modified external tank suite struts. As on most other missions, the Night Stalkers helicopters had a double 7.62-mm machine-gun pod on the right rack with a twelve-tube 2.75-inch rocket launcher pod next to it; on the left of the helicopter Oz climbed into was a 532 countermeasure dispenser to defeat heat-seeking as well as radar-guided missiles, with the last position on the strut occupied by four Hellfire missiles like those the Apaches carried.

The door gunners on each side of the helicopters manned four-barrel 7.62-mm Miniguns that could be aimed at targets on either side of the aircraft. These automatic weapons were capable of laying down a withering fire, quickly suppressing enemy ground troops.

Both the Apaches and MH-60Ks had been designed for survivability. Their wide-spaced engines had infrared-filtering nacelles, minimizing the chances of both being knocked out by heavy ground fire or hit by heat-seeking rockets. Redundant systems spaced throughout the chopper along with Kevlar and titanium armor enabled them to withstand intense small-arms fire.

The marines mounting the MH-60Ks carried a variety of weapons including Colt M16A2 rifles, M203 grenade launchers, Colt M16 H-BARs that served as squad automatic weapons or sniper rifles, and M60 light machine guns. In addition to their primary weapons, the soldiers carried stun and fragmentation grenades, M9 bayonets, and K-Bar, Ek, or other custom fighting knives. Lieutenant Vasco and his sergeants also carried silenced Ruger Mark II pistols designed for dealing quietly with sentries or guard dogs. All the marines carried night vision goggles and traveled light, with a minimum of gear to hamper their movements when they reached the island.

Oz settled into his bucket seat on the left of the cockpit, fastened his shoulder harness, then snapped his helmet mike into the intercom system. "Let's get this bird wound up," he told his copilot.

Oz checked the positional lights, or slimes on the Apache ahead of him, saw them glowing brightly in his night vision goggles, and adjusted his heading ever so slightly with a sideward nudge of the control column in his right hand. The choppers flew at 300 feet in a trail formation, snaking behind each other with an AH-64 at the head and tail of the group. Their low altitude, coupled with the "stealth" paint on the helicopters, minimized the chances of radar detection, although there had been no sign of radar as they neared Kakira.

Death Song took a reading of his gyromagnetic compass. "Right on course, Captain."

The pilot glanced at his twin screens to check the displays and then looked through his chin window at the waves that hurtled past. He scanned upward at the stars twinkling radiantly in a cloudless night, magnified to bright points of light by his night vision goggles until they became tiny will-of-the-wisps that seemed to chase along with the helicopter.

O.T. and Luger sat in silence at their Miniguns, which had been rotated out of their storage compartments and now protruded from the side windows through which the warm tropical air whistled, filling the helicopter with the smell of the sea.

The pilot checked the screen in front of him again. "I'm reading twenty kilometers to the northeast shore of Kakira."

"That's a roger," Death Song agreed. "We're at checkpoint Alpha."

"Get us connected to Warner," the pilot directed.

Death Song switched on their radio, a modified AN/ASC-15B triservice battlefield support system that uplinked to a military communications satellite orbiting above them. The satellite accepted the onboard computer's ID code and then relayed their signal to another satellite above the United States. From there the signal was transferred to earth and routed to Fort Bragg. "You're on line," Death Song announced when the light on the panel flashed green.

"This is Avenging Storm One," Oz said over the radio link. "Can you read us?"

"That's a roger," Warner answered, his voice sounding metallic in the radio interference of the thick Pacific air. "How are things progressing? Over."

"We're at checkpoint Alpha, and await confirmation to continue, over," Oz responded, his muscles tensing in the darkness as he wondered if the mission might be aborted at the last minute.

"You have a go-ahead, I say again, go ahead. Verify."

"I verify," Oz replied. "We have a go-ahead and will continue our mission. Over."

"Good luck, Avenging Storm One, over and out."

The pilot clicked his radio to the ultrahigh frequency of the battle net used to communicate between his helicopters. "Okay, gang, we've received the go-ahead. Go in hot but remember we don't want any firing unless we're having trouble extracting the marines. Stick to the flight program unless we run into problems. We will descend to thirty meters now."

Oz lowered the collective pitch lever in his left fist, dropping the chopper in a giddy fall along with those behind and in front of him. The pilot ignored the vertical situation display and watched out the window instead, since such low altitudes were within the error range of his instruments. He eased up on the collective when he'd reached thirty meters; now the six aircraft almost skimmed the dark water that was painted green and white by his night vision goggles. At such a low altitude, the chances of detection even by radar were minimal.

He switched to his intercom. "Lieutenant Vasco, we're nearing the island."

"We'll be ready when you get there," the marine answered over his headset.

"O.T. and Luger," Oz called. "Open the side doors."

"We've got 'em," O.T. answered. Then there

were twin clicks on the intercom as the two gunners removed their helmet mikes from the system and headed back to open the sliding hatches on either side of the MH-60K.

Oz surveyed the rolling waves on the ocean's surface, piling up in the shallows over a reef north of the island. The wind kicked the helicopter for a moment and stirred the waves below. The pilot quickly compensated with his control column, bringing them back onto course.

The intercom clicked twice, telling him the gunners were reconnecting into the intercom, and then O.T. spoke. "Our side doors are open and ready for the marines to exit when we touch down."

Oz glanced over at Death Song. The navigator stared at the horizontal situation display, then tapped a key on the chopper's computer console. "There's our LZ," Death Song said, highlighting the position on the screen in front of the pilot. "You're X-ringing it. Still no sign of enemy radar or radio communication. If there's anyone down there, they aren't using their electronics."

Oz double-checked the glowing HSD and then spoke over the intercom. "Lieutenant Vasco, we're approaching the LZ. Everything's quiet and there's no sign of anyone ahead of us."

For a moment the pilot wondered why any group powerful enough to take on an American Coast Guard cutter wouldn't be using radar, and then his thoughts were interrupted by Vasco's voice: "We're lock-and-loading our firearms now. We're ready to kick some ass."

"Activate our weapons systems," Oz ordered

his crew. "Just remember that we're *not* to fire unless fired on."

"That's a roger," O.T. said.

"Roger," Luger echoed.

"You have the machine-gun pod and rockets," Death Song informed the pilot. "I'll retain control of the Hellfires."

The low peaks of Kakira loomed ahead of them, surrounded by light clouds tinted white and green by the night vision goggles. The six helicopters approached the northeast side of the island opposite the natural harbor where the two ships rested.

Oz glanced at the HSD and clicked on his radio. "Let's reduce speed to one-twenty kph." He watched the slimes of the Apache ahead of him, carefully slowing to match its speed by pulling the control column backward. The formation of helicopters decelerated to one hundred twenty kilometers per hour on their approach to the island, the aircraft still skimming above the water that lifted and rolled beneath them.

Because the fortifications on the island were concentrated along the beaches, Oz had decided to take Ensign Addis's suggestion to simply leapfrog the barriers, dropping the marines onto the plateau in the central region of the island. While most of the trenches around the island interconnected, the section facing the sheer cliffs along the northern shore was notably devoid of defenses. The Americans had plotted a course that would weave around most of the trenches and would allow them, they hoped, to avoid being detected by whoever held the island.

As the column of helicopters neared the narrow beach, the rolling waves kicked white foam over the sand. Abruptly the Apache ahead of Oz leaped skyward to clear the rocky face ahead of them, and the pilot yanked on his collective pitch lever to climb, mimicking the flight of the chopper ahead of him.

The crew and passengers were shoved into their seats as the G forces mounted, the cliff face growing until it appeared the MH-60K would smash against it. But the chopper passed above the rocks, then dropped downward in a giddy fall, following a twisting stream that wove its way through the volcanic rock. The thumping of the helicopter rotors reverberated along the narrow valley as the string of aircraft resumed their nap-of-the-earth course.

"There's our SP," Death Song warned, double-checking the screens in front of him to be sure he hadn't mistaken the tall rock that served as his reference. The SP, or start point, was the beginning of the winding run that led to the landing zone where the four MH-60Ks would land and the marines would disembark.

"AS Two and Six," Oz called on the radio. "Time to peel off."

The Apaches at either end of the column shot to the side, adopting paths that would allow them to orbit the landing site in an overwatch and security flight, supplying suppressive fire if it was needed.

Oz was now in the lead position, with the other three MH-60Ks behind him. He concentrated on the rocky path ahead as they progressed toward their objective.

"LZ dead ahead," Death Song told the pilot. "Fifty meters."

"Anybody see anything?" the pilot asked his crew.

"Negative on starboard," Luger answered.

"Looks clear," O.T. agreed. "Side doors are secured."

"Nothing but our people on the FLIR," Death Song said.

Oz toggled on his radio. "Looks cold and we're heading down," he informed the pilots behind him. He pulled back on the control column, causing the chopper to nose upward and bleed its airspeed for the approach. The MH-60K's velocity continued to drop as the airman lowered the collective pitch lever until the helicopter skimmed the rocky plateau ahead, its wheels skipping along the stones while ground effect bounced the aircraft upward. "How do things look up there, Two?"

The voice of the Apache pilot answered, "Looks clear."

Nearing his landing position, Oz depressed the collective, bringing the helicopter low enough that the wheels rolled along the bumpy surface. "How's it look, Six?" he asked the second Apache.

"Looks cold from here."

Satisfied it was safe, Oz swiftly depressed the lever to anchor them on the earth. The helicopter came to a complete halt, and the pilot said nothing over the intercom, knowing his passengers would exit without the need to order them to do so. He watched as the marines scampered toward the jungle foliage around them. This was the time the helicopters were most vulnerable to attack, and the pilot felt his pulse pounding.

Sitting ducks, Oz thought. "Anybody see anything?" he asked his crew over the intercom.

"Still negative," Luger answered.

"Looks clear," O.T. agreed. "Passengers are all out and side doors are secured."

"Nothing but our people on the FLIR," Death Song said.

Oz nervously tapped the collective pitch lever and waited. Now the helicopter crews would have to sit tight and hope no one spotted them. *And that's not the easiest thing in the world to do*, he thought, searching the area around the aircraft to be sure it was free of any sign of enemy soldiers.

He watched as the last of the marines melted into the vegetation and vanished into the darkness.

CHAPTER

18

"Get in here, Cox," Johnson whispered to his helper. The engineer listened in the darkness as the sailor stumbled into the galley. "And get away from the hatchway," he added, bringing up his rifle and wishing he could see something in the pitch black interior of the ship.

The two sailors heard the faint patter of someone stealthily walking down the passageway outside the galley. As he listened, Johnson found himself breathing as softly as he could, half fearful that whoever was in the corridor might hear him, even though he knew that was impossible.

The soft noise of leather against the deck continued until the individual was alongside the open hatch. He paused and all was silent.

Damn, Johnson thought. *I should have had Cox close it like it was when we got here.* But it was too late now to do anything.

He continued to listen and heard whoever was outside step into the galley, the scrape of metal against the bulkhead—undoubtedly a rifle—announcing his presence in the room.

The engineer could stand the tension no longer. He rose in the darkness, his finger tightening on the trigger of his rifle as he switched on the light with his off hand, bathing the intruder in a cone of light. "Fernandez!" Johnson gasped, his finger nearly pulling on the trigger before he recognized the sailor. "What the hell are you doing here?"

"I thought maybe something had happened to you—you've been gone so long. I just thought—"

"Shit!" Cox hissed. "We could have shot you, man."

"You were to stay put," Johnson agreed. "I just about blew your fool head off." The engineer took a deep breath, his hands shaking from the adrenaline coursing through his veins. "Close the hatch behind you and help us get some of this food carted back to our hideout," he finally said. "And next time I tell you to stay put, you *do* it!"

"I will," the sailor promised and then turned to close the hatch.

"Cox," the engineer said, "give me one of the bags you brought with you." He pushed his rifle across his back and laid the flashlight on a nearby counter so he could see.

The sailor handed Johnson an empty laundry bag, and the engineer opened it and crossed to the treasure trove of gourmet food he'd uncovered, carefully dropping the cans, jars, and packets into it. Shrimp, caviar, tins of biscuits—all went into the bag, along with items Johnson didn't recognize or whose labels were printed in foreign languages.

Ravindran will kill me when he finds out I

cleaned out his stores, the engineer thought with a grin. Then he realized that chances were good he'd never even see Ravindran again. In fact it was probable he was dead. *What a mess.*

He dropped another tin into the sack and hefted it. *Better not try to get any more in it or the bottom will rip out,* he decided. "All right," he said, turning back toward Cox. "Take this and give me the other bag. We might as well carry everything we can so we don't have to do this again for a while. Fernandez, grab some of those bottles of wine down there."

The sailors did as the engineer ordered, and within three minutes Johnson had filled the second sack as full as he thought he could without risking its splitting open. He slung the heavy sack over his shoulder, smiling to himself as he pictured the Santa Claus image he likely presented. He pulled his rifle around on its sling so it was under his right arm and then picked up the flashlight from the counter. "Okay. Let's be real careful," he told the sailors. "And don't let the bottles clank together," he added, still feeling angry with Fernandez for coming after him and nearly getting his fool head blown off.

The three men crossed to the hatchway, and Johnson switched off the flashlight and placed it in his back pocket. Then he checked his front pocket to be sure the spare rifle magazine was still waiting there. "Let's go," he ordered.

The three carefully stepped into the blackened passageway and started toward the stairs that led to the engine room. The sound of voices drifted toward them.

Johnson froze as he saw the glimmer of light ahead of him; Fernandez plowed into him and dropped one of the bottles of wine he carried, the glass shattering on the metal deck, the echo rumbling down the passageway.

The light ahead of the three Americans went out, and then a bright flash lit the darkness. A bullet careened past Johnson's head, and then a deafening roar filled the corridor. The engineer dropped the bag he carried and brought his rifle up, flattening himself against the bulkhead as a second bullet zinged past him.

"Cox, Fernandez, hold your fire," he ordered, fearful the two sailors behind him might shoot him accidentally in the darkness. "Just stay down. They seem to be aiming high."

He dropped to his knee, gritting his teeth as a shard of glass cut into it. Raising his Kalashnikov, he clicked off the safety and then mashed the trigger.

The automatic rifle rattled in his hands, spitting fire that lit up the targets ahead of him. The muzzle climbed as the gun continued to fire, hitting the deck ahead of the engineer since he had purposely aimed low, then climbing as the recoil raised the barrel. The American watched as the bullets smacked into the three Japanese running toward him, their rifles held forward in a futile bayonet charge.

Abruptly the corridor was plunged into darkness as the rifle exhausted its magazine. All Johnson heard was the bell-like tones of the empty brass cartridges that had been expelled from his gun rolling across the deck.

"What's going on?" Fernandez asked from behind him.

Johnson half choked in the acrid smoke left behind from his volley as he rose to his feet. He frantically released the magazine from his rifle and jammed the metal box into his front pocket. "I got them all," he told his men, reaching into his pocket, extracting his only spare magazine and rocking it into the rifle. He awkwardly searched for the charging lever and, finding it, pulled it back and let go, loading the rifle.

"We better hurry and get out of here," Cox whispered nervously.

"Yeah, right," Johnson agreed. "Pick up the bags and let's go. Be careful up here. There're three bodies between us and the stairs. Watch your step so you don't trip over them."

The engineer held the bag and the flashlight in his left hand, awkwardly turning it on while he held his rifle at the ready at his side where it rested on its sling. He glanced at the Japanese soldiers he'd downed and choked down the acid taste of vomit.

The three sailors hurried down the hall and stepped over the fallen Japanese. Johnson forced himself to avoid looking closely at the shattered bodies he passed, nearly gagging again at the pools of blood forming on the deck. He clicked off his flashlight once they were past the corpses and continued down the passageway, slowing when he felt they were nearing the stairs. Then he paused to snap on his flashlight and stepped to the edge of the stairway before turning the light off.

The engineer froze, hearing footsteps echoing in the dark corridor behind them. "Fernandez, Cox, get to either side of the passage and let me stand between you; maybe we can handle these guys with our combined firepower."

Johnson lowered his bag to the top step, then turned and positioned himself between the two sailors. He raised his rifle, squinting in the darkness in an effort to see his opponents. "Fire short bursts to keep the rifle from climbing," the engineer whispered to the two men on either side of him. "Otherwise you'll waste your shots."

Tricky bastards, Johnson thought, as he strained to hear whoever was creeping down the hall. He heard the faint squeak of a boot and scrape of metal on the bulkhead. *They've almost reached the three we downed,* he realized. That would be a good time to fire at them, while they were trying to figure out who was lying dead in the blackened passageway.

"Get ready," Johnson whispered, feeling the side of the receiver on his rifle, checking that the safety was switched to automatic fire. "Don't shoot until I do," he cautioned the two sailors.

The men ahead of him spoke Japanese so softly he could barely hear them. *Found the bodies,* Johnson told himself. He mashed the trigger of his rifle, and a long round of automatic fire burst from the muzzle of his weapon, the blast echoing through the passage and spitting fire that lit the four soldiers ahead of him.

The two sailors on either side of the engineer joined in the fusillade, sending more bullets crack-

ing down the narrow corridor. The projectiles ricocheted off the metal bulkhead and flashed into the
darkness.

In the muzzle flashes, Johnson watched the
four Japanese soldiers fall into a tangled mass on
top of the three who had already been killed.
Seeing them downed, Johnson quit firing, as did
Fernandez. Cox continued to pump his trigger,
sending more bullets snapping down the passageway and lighting the dead troopers with a strobing
flash.

"Cease firing," Johnson hollered at Cox.
"They're all down. Come on, let's get out of here."
The engineer grabbed the flashlight from his pocket and flicked it on, turning to retrieve his bag and
head down the stairwell.

"Watch your step," he cautioned and then he
froze. A movement at the base of the steps had
caught his eye. In horror, he saw a Japanese soldier
step into the beam of the flashlight; the trooper
raised an M60 machine gun and pulled the trigger,
climbing the stairs toward the Americans as he
fired.

The bullets clanged against the bulkhead
around Johnson and smashed into his chest and
arms. The engineer fell backward, his flashlight
falling to the deck and rolling to a stop against the
wall.

Another volley from the stairs downed both
Fernandez and Cox, who cried out in pain and
dropped beside the engineer. Johnson tried to
crawl toward his rifle, only to discover his legs
refused to work. He closed his eyes and lay motion-

less, then raised himself on his arms to watch the soldier climb the last of the steps, the muzzle of his weapon covering the three fallen sailors.

In the dim light from the flashlight that rested on the deck, Johnson saw the Japanese trooper carefully aim at the unconscious Fernandez. The enemy soldier smiled and pulled the trigger, pumping a string of bullets into the man and splattering the walls of the passageway with blood.

The muzzle turned to Cox, who moaned softly as he watched; the gun spit fire and slugs, smashing his head to pulp.

The machine gun turned toward Johnson.

"Go to hell, you stupid bastard," the engineer taunted the soldier. "You dumb slug, don't you know the war's over? You guys got to lose twice before it counts or what?"

The soldier said nothing. The machine gun from the Coast Guard cutter clattered, and Johnson was dead.

19

Lieutenant Vasco studied the tall palms and scrub brush through his night vision goggles for a couple of seconds, then signaled his column to continue its advance. The enemy was undoubtedly on the island, but finding a spot to ambush them was going to be tricky, especially since it was likely some of the enemy stationed in the perimeter trenches heard the helicopters on the way in to the center of the island.

Vasco kept his rifle strapped across his back and held his silenced Ruger .22 pistol in his fist, ready to fire if necessary. While the .22 slugs from the self-loading handgun weren't highly lethal, he was a crack shot, and the advantage of being able to fire without disturbing everyone on the island made the weapon ideal for a mission like this one.

The lieutenant had left two squads behind to guard the choppers; his squad then went out to capture prisoners to carry back to Guam for questioning. With the modern drugs and techniques that the Americans were able to employ, Vasco was sure their prisoners would be talking freely in a short time, filling in all the holes in the information the military had about the island.

The squad advanced cautiously, each marine watching either side of the tree-lined footpath for any sign of the enemy. The soldiers' faces were covered with death masks of camouflage paint, and the night vision goggles and plastic helmets they wore made them appear more like machines than men. Advancing slowly down the winding trail, they had been forced to travel single file rather than in the safer double wedge formation they normally adopted.

The lieutenant glanced toward the thick brush to either side, leery of an ambush, but he knew from the aerial photos that at least no guardposts were located along the trail. *I hope no one's put in any new ones since then*, he added to himself, creeping forward with his men.

Every few minutes Vasco pivoted his tall, muscular frame around to check the progress of his men on the trail behind him. He turned back to see the point man give a signal and the column stopped; the point man signaled again and the squad crept into the foliage screening the high side of the path, blending into the plants to become invisible.

Vasco turned from his hiding position and peered around the palm between him and the pathway. The trail was empty; then he heard the faint sound of voices. He listened and recognized the language.

Japanese, he thought with surprise. *Damned if they aren't speaking Japanese.*

But that didn't mean there really were Japanese troops left over from World War II, he tried to reassure himself; it had to be a coincidence. Maybe they were simply Japanese terrorists who had studied old military manuals. *We'll know soon enough if we can capture one of them*, he promised himself, ignoring the mosquito that buzzed near his right ear. In the distance a bird cried in the night, and then the jungle was quiet. The lieutenant squinted toward the bend in the brush-covered trail ahead of him.

Still nothing.

Beside the lieutenant one of his machine gunners carrying an M60 carefully straightened out the belt of the weapon. Recently modified to the E2 configuration, the gun had a forward pistol grip under its barrel. Satisfied the belt was as it should be, the soldier rested the M60 in the fork of a dead tree and pivoted the machine gun so it covered the path. On the other side of the officer, an M203 grenadier knelt and prepared his launcher.

The lieutenant turned his attention back toward the trail. Four shabby soldiers sauntered around the bend, their rifles slung over their shoulders with the stocks hanging behind them, each holding his firearm by the barrel that projected ahead of him. The men traveled slowly, obviously blinded by the thick darkness of the jungle.

Vasco turned toward the grenadier standing beside him. "Come onto the trail with me."

"Yes, sir," the soldier responded, nervously fingering his weapon.

The two Americans pushed their way onto the dark path. Vasco transferred his pistol to his left hand and removed the heavy aluminum flashlight from his belt, gripping its long tube like a club.

The Japanese soldiers continued toward the

men, unable to see them in the gloom. Only when the four soldiers were nearly on top of the two Americans did one of them see the marines blocking their way.

The Japanese soldier came to a standstill, the man beside him continuing forward while the soldier behind him plowed into his back and muttered an oath when the butt of the rifle caught him in the teeth.

Before the Japanese soldiers could react further, Vasco stepped forward and slammed his flashlight across the temple of the trooper in front of him, instantly downing the soldier. The lieutenant's second blow failed to connect as the Japanese he aimed for pulled back and attempted to bring his rifle into play.

Vasco quickly dropped his flashlight and transfered his pistol to his right hand, bringing it up and thumbing off its safety the same instant the Japanese rifleman fired blindly into the darkness.

The bullet missed the two marines by a wide margin, the muzzle flash illuminating the jungle like lightning when amplified by the NVG Vasco wore. The lieutenant ignored the noise and flame and cooly pumped three slugs from his Ruger into the soldier; the Japanese tumbled into a pile.

Vasco turned to engage the other two soldiers, who had turned to run, but saw them stumble and fall, the victims of the hail of bullets that came from the silenced gun of his sergeant. After the brief flurry of clattering as the two silenced pistols cycled, the jungle was ominously silent.

Holding his pistol ready, Vasco knelt and felt the neck of the man he'd coldcocked. The vein in his neck beat beneath the officer's fingertips. "O'Conner, Karr," Vasco ordered, rising to his feet. "You two come down here and get this sucker. Looks like we have our prisoner."

The two marines silently stepped onto the trail and knelt to pick up the unconscious Japanese prisoner. "Gee, Lieutenant," one of the marines muttered as they hoisted the unconscious man between them, "why didn't you conk one of the little guys instead of the biggest mother in the lot?"

"You need the exercise, marine," Vasco answered. "Now let's get a move on before his *big* brothers come around to see what all the commotion was about."

"Yes, sir."

The column rapidly retraced its steps, the Americans knowing that the discharge of the Japanese soldier's rifle would soon attract unwanted attention. As they retreated toward their choppers, Vasco removed the AN/PRT-4 radio from its pouch and flipped it on. "AS One, this is Ground One, can you read me?"

"Roger, G One," Oz's voice replied over the radio.

"We have a bird in hand and are headed in. ETA fifteen minutes."

"We'll be ready to go when you get here."

"Over and out," Vasco finished, clicking off his radio and replacing it in its pouch.

The soldiers continued forward, the point man creeping cautiously like a wild animal, ever wary of a trap. Vasco glanced toward the hill above them and saw a flicker of movement. He pivoted on the balls of his feet, drawing his Mark II pistol from its holster and instantly aligning its sights on his target in one fluid motion. Without thinking, he felt his finger squeezing the weapon's trigger three times.

There was the quick popping of three bullets leaving the barrel and a faint thumping when they stitched the form of a Japanese soldier half hidden in a tall elephant plant. The three empty cartridges ejected from Vasco's firearm tinkled in the sand, and then all was quiet.

The point man's rifle exploded and was quickly accompanied by the heavy thumps of the marines' M60 machine gun and other rifles. Instead of looking toward the points where the soldiers aimed, Vasco scanned the side of the trail, looking for other possible targets.

As he searched, another shape sprang out of nowhere on the slope, half hidden by a bush, his bolt-action rifle aimed toward the trail.

"Heads up!" Vasco yelled to his squad as he spotted two more enemy troops beside the first. "Above us." He fired his Ruger at one of the forms and was satisfied to see his target drop.

The marine machine gunners raked the other two soldiers with fire while his riflemen sent three-round bursts toward their other foes. Within moments of the first shots, the last of the enemy troops was riddled and had dropped from sight.

"Watch both sides of the trail!" Vasco ordered the men behind him as he holstered his pistol; there was no longer any need for a silenced weapon. He removed the rifle from his shoulder as the column resumed its march toward the helicopters.

They had traveled fifty paces when four more of

the enemy sprang up on the slope below them. Vasco lifted his rifle, throttling the trigger as he centered the rifle's sights on one of the figures; bullets erupted from his Colt carbine and smashed into the Japanese soldier. Without waiting for his foe to drop, the lieutenant shifted his aim, and three more projectiles crashed into his next target as the machine guns and rifles in the squad barked a loud accompaniment to his firearm.

The four shapes disappeared into the foliage as quickly as they had appeared.

"Don't bunch up," the sergeant behind Vasco ordered the marines.

The lieutenant faced forward to see his point man punch the magazine release of his rifle and quickly reload it before resuming his progression along the trail.

Vasco raised his NVG, startled at how dark it was without the instrument, and wiped the sweat from his eyes before lowering it again. The acrid smell of gunsmoke hung in the air and burned his nostrils as he proceeded forward on the ominously quiet hillside.

This is going to get real tricky from here on out, the marine thought as he signaled his men to keep moving forward.

"They're where?" Major Tashida asked incredulously.

"On the ridge near the *jinja*," the breathless messenger answered.

"So the perimeter guards were right," Tashida

said, half to himself. Some strange type of quiet aircraft had flown toward the center of the island.
What could intruders be doing there? He decided he
would worry about that later. Now they were defil-
ing the holy place of his *kami*—that in itself was
enough to make him furious. "Who's on watch on
the northern slope?" the major asked, turning
toward his aide.

"Lieutenant Ishimoto," the young man
answered.

The major looked back to his messenger. "Tell
Ishimoto to move his forces up the northern paths.
I'll bring two platoons up the southern slope of the
ridge. Be sure he takes some of the new rockets
with him. Hurry."

"*Hai,*" the messenger barked, bowing and then
running from the room.

Tashida took his sword from its *katanakake*
stand, shoved the bladed weapon into his belt, and
then tapped the Nambu pistol at his side to be sure
it was there. "Come on," he ordered his aide.
"Perhaps we will finally be able to fight these cow-
ardly Americans in a real battle of steel against
steel."

The marines moved quickly along the jungle trail
and encountered no resistance until they were only
a few minutes away from the pickup zone. They
traveled quickly, not nearly as cautious as before,
since they knew the longer they took the more apt
the Japanese soldiers were to converge on the area
and trap them. Vasco saw the point man kneel; the

lieutenant raised his hand to indicate a halt, dropping to one knee.

The point man signaled, and the squad crashed into the jungle around them, then stood still. Four seconds after the marines had vanished from the pathway, the voices of Japanese soldiers accompanied by the clanking of their equipment announced their advance up the footpath as they searched for the Americans.

Vasco waited until the enemy soldiers were alongside his men and yelled his order: "Fire."

The woods blazed with an inferno of gunfire and grenades for fifteen seconds. Then the din abruptly ceased when the twelve Japanese soldiers on the pathway had tumbled to the sand, dead or dying. The lieutenant rose and started for the trail, when the point man frantically signaled. More troops were coming.

Only now they know right where we are, Vasco thought dismally. The noise of a man approaching through the foliage caused the officer to turn. "What have you got?" he whispered to the marine sergeant.

"We've got a bunch of guys coming up behind us," the sergeant answered. "Sounds like they heard our shooting and know about where we are."

Trapped! Vasco thought, reaching for his radio.

20

"AS One," Lieutenant Vasco's voice called over the radio. "They have us pinned down."

Oz toggled his transmitter on. "Where are you, Ground One?"

"Hard to say in this overgrowth. Maybe one click from you. Probably less."

"Hang on and I'll get some firepower to you. Where're the bad guys from your position?"

"On either side of us, north and south. Got to sign off—we're taking fire. Hurry up with the cavalry."

Oz flipped to the air battle net frequency and called the pilots in the two Apaches circling the area. "AS Two and Six, Ground One has run into some trouble. They're about one click from the PZ, cornered with bad guys front and back. Think you can handle it?"

"That's a roger," the pilot of Two replied.

"AS One," the other called. "This is Six. We just spotted a big party coming up the hill toward you. About four minutes away at the rate they're climbing. Want me to trash them?"

"That's a roger, Six," Oz answered. "Hit them

hard and then follow Two to help Ground One."

"Got it, One."

Oz took a deep breath and then spoke again. "AS Three, Four, and Five. Looks like the bad guys figured out where we were headed. We've got them coming up from the north. We'd better get the marines around the PZ on board ASAP." Without waiting for a reply, he snapped over to the marine channel. "Ground One, come in please."

"This is Ground One, over."

"Help is headed your way, but we've got bad guys on the ground near the PZ. I suggest we load your men here on the birds so we can hightail it in a hurry if we need to."

"That's a roger," Vasco agreed. "I'll give the order to my people. I can hear one of your choppers coming up now. Ground One out."

Within moments, Vasco had radioed the men around the four grounded helicopters, ordering them back to the aircraft. Oz watched the marines charging toward the MH-60Ks behind him; none entered the chopper Oz piloted, since Vasco and the squad he was with would board it when they returned.

Four explosions rocked the jungle, and an Apache thundered overhead, its pilot intent on attacking the Japanese ground forces. Oz watched the aircraft and then lost it behind the dense tree line along the ridge.

Within ten seconds the three MH-60Ks on the ground behind Oz reported that they were ready for takeoff. "All right," he told the pilots on the other choppers. "Stand by for takeoff while One and Six clear the way for Ground One."

* * *

Lieutenant Ishimoto raised his missile tube and centered the Apache thundering overhead in its crosshairs, feeling in awe of the magnificent machine that flitted through the air like a giant wraith, killing most of his soldiers on the trail in a matter of seconds with its heavy machine gun and rockets.

The aircraft slowed to a near stop above the trail in front of Ishimoto, its chin gun spitting fire into the darkness beyond, drowning out the fearful shouts of Ishimoto's men and the cries of the dying. The Japanese lieutenant's finger squeezed the trigger of the launcher and a missile hissed out, riding on a tail of flame toward the almost stationary Apache above him.

The warhead of the rocket collided with the lower side of the helicopter, exploding in its port engine. Within a fraction of a second the fuel tank erupted into a ball of fire and the twisting wreckage sank into the foliage and exploded again, showering blazing fragments into the jungle around Ishimoto.

The Japanese soldier bent and removed another rocket launcher from the back of the dead soldier beside him.

I will be ready for the next flying machine that comes this way.

"One," the frantic pilot of the second Apache called as he raced toward the position where the American chopper had just gone down. "Two has been hit. Crashed and burned—I doubt there are any survivors."

"I read you, Six," Oz radioed back. "Better keep moving—sounds like they have AA."

"That's a roger, One. My FLIR shows another band of soldiers coming through the jungle directly for you. Want me to take them?"

"Negative, Six," Oz called. "Head for Ground One and cut them loose."

"Roger, One."

"Three, Four, and Five," Oz called to the grounded MH-60Ks behind him. "We've got company coming. Take your choppers and head north back to home base," he continued, lifting on the collective pitch lever. His chopper rose into the air, bouncing on the ground effect blast coming up from the earth below. "I want you to travel at minimum speed so I can call you back if I need to," he told the pilots in the helicopters behind him.

"Three taking off now."

"Four headed up."

"Five bringing up the rear and headed home."

Oz wheeled his chopper southward as the MH-60Ks behind him peeled onto an opposite heading. He was about to radio the remaining Apache when the pilot's frantic voice called: "We've got a rocket on our tail. Can't seem to shake it—"

A brilliant explosion rocked the night and the radio fell silent.

Oz knew the Apache had been hit. He was silent for a moment as he traveled toward the position where Vasco's men were pinned down. "Anything on radar?" he finally asked.

"Negative," Death Song replied. "And no enemy radio traffic—they must have ground lines."

The pilot shoved down on the collective pitch lever to skim the bank of trees ahead of him as he raced toward the marine position. The chopper plunged over the hill ahead, weaving above the trail leading to the American troops. The flashes of small arms lit the trail, followed by the clatter of bullets on the exterior of the aircraft.

"I've got 'em," O.T.'s voice hollered on the intercom. The flash of the four spinning barrels of his Minigun lit the side of the chopper as the gunner raked the brush below.

The pilot skimmed over a tall palm tree, the tail of the chopper snipping the fronds as they passed.

"There's Ground One at one o'clock," Death Song reported. "Looks like they're still pinned down."

Oz rocked the chopper forward, aligning the nose of the MH-60K on the knot of enemy soldiers behind the marines. His finger stabbed the red button on the control column, sending three Hydra 70 rockets hissing from the tubes on the side of the helicopter.

A machine-gun lit the jungle below the chopper, sending tracers streaming past the nose of the aircraft; the ground fire abruptly ended as Luger's Minigun came to bear on the enemy position.

A moment later the rockets Oz had launched reached their target, creating fiery blasts that transformed the night into day. The helicopter raced over the enemy position, its blades whipping the rising smoke into twirling loops as it passed.

Oz circled the trail, his machine-gun pod rattling as he sighted targets of opportunity, while the Miniguns on either side of the aircraft created a deadly accompaniment to his fire.

Luger mashed the dual triggers on his weapon, bathing the squad of Japanese troops half hidden in the jungle with fire. The chopper glided past, and the gunner spotted a distant flash that he had no trouble recognizing.

"Missile," Luger hollered on the intercom. "At five o'clock coming up fast."

Abruptly the helicopter banked to the left as the pilot attempted to lose the rocket bearing down on them. Luger watched in horror as the missile mimicked their turn, speeding up to reduce the distance between it and the aircraft while ignoring the bright burning flare that Death Song had released behind them in an effort to throw the projectile off their trail.

The missile was almost on top of them when the helicopter roared over the edge of the ridge and dropped earthward, causing the gunner to hang weightless in his harness. He held the edge of the side port, craning his head out the opening to stare upward. The missile raced past them, seeming to miss the rotors above him by only inches.

Luger swallowed and then spoke over the intercom. "They missed us by a hair. Didn't look like the flare had any effect on it—and it was definitely guided."

"Glad you spotted it," the pilot replied. "You guys keep a sharp lookout back there."

"Don't worry," O.T. said. "We don't want to make you look bad by getting blown out of the sky."

Oz yanked upward on the collective pitch lever, sending the MH-60K bounding back over the ridge, returning them to the enemy soldiers who still had Ground One pinned down.

"There's a knot of men along the trail toward starboard," Death Song warned. "At four o'clock."

"I see them," Luger answered, his voice emotionless as he thumbed the triggers of his weapon. The flaming salvo lit the side of the chopper as Oz pushed it forword.

The flash of a machine gun lit up the path ahead of the helicopter, and the pilot nosed the chopper down, firing his machine guns while O.T.'s Minigun blasted the jungle beside them with a long string of thunder.

"Another rocket launcher at twelve o'clock," Death Song warned.

"Got it," Oz said, spotting the soldier lifting the launch tube. The pilot jabbed his rocket launch button, and the pod alongside the MH-60K ejected a 70-mm missile that streamed toward the target. Oz kicked his left rudder pedal and climbed above the path as his rocket reached its target, ripping through the jungle and blowing the launcher and its operator to bits.

As the pilot traversed the jungle, he was able to gain a better view of the battle unfolding below. The marines were pinned down by the fire from the trail and ridge above them. "I'm going to pass over the enemy at the north end of the trail," he alerted his crew. "Let's see if we can clean their clocks."

Oz watched the telltale flashes from the muzzles of enemy rifles as he dived toward the Japanese on the trail. The staccato discharges were accompanied by the snapping of bullets against the underside of the chopper. Ignoring them, the pilot brought the aircraft into alignment with the troops, shoving the fire button with his thumb. The .30-caliber guns in the pod expelled their deadly fusillade, and tracers arched along the path, knocking over the gunners below him.

The Miniguns on both side of the chopper spit death as he wheeled for another pass, again dropping the chopper below the ridge to minimize his exposure to missiles. As he turned the MH-60K, the machine leaped over the ridge and hurtled down the path.

He hit the launch button with his little finger, sending a long salvo of rockets streaming toward the north end of the trail. The projectiles crossed the space to the ground in seconds and exploded with furious bursts that threw men, dirt, and foliage in all directions.

"Ground fire is dropping off," O.T. reported while Oz circled back to see if another attack was needed. "Just a few sporadic rifles from the looks of it."

Oz clicked on his radio. "Ground One, how are you holding up down there?"

"Pretty well. Looks like you got just about everyone in front of us."

"It's better than it was, but there're still a few up

ahead of you. If you can head for the PZ, we can pin down the clowns on your tail."

"Roger that," Vasco answered. "We'll start for the PZ. Over and out."

"Okay guys," Oz said to his crew. "Keep the enemy occupied so the marines can get out."

The American troops quickly advanced to the pickup zone, dealing with the Japanese stragglers who had survived the earlier massive attack by the American helicopters.

"We're ready and waiting at the PZ," Vasco's voice finally called to Oz.

"We're heading for you now," the pilot answered.

Within moments the MH-60K was over the marines. Satisfied the area was clear, Oz lowered the collective pitch lever and aligned his aircraft so its nose was pointed south as it had been when the marines had exited the chopper. He depressed the collective pitch lever with his left hand, and the helicopter dropped to the ground so fast it bounced on its hydraulic struts.

The squad of marines raced out of the darkness to climb aboard, two of the troopers carrying an unconscious form between them.

Is he worth the death of four American airmen? Oz wondered, studying the small Japanese prisoner and recalling the men he had lost in the Apache crashes. He hoped the information they got from the prisoner would be of value.

"They're all aboard," O.T. shouted, and the pilot

felt the vibrations within the air frame as the gunners slid the side doors shut.

Oz lifted the MH-60K into the air, kicked a rudder pedal to counter the gust that threw them to the side, and toggled his radio on. "Three, Four, and Five, we're coming up behind you. We should catch up in a few minutes. Maintain minimum speed until we do. Over and out."

Oz eased the control column forward, picking up speed as they leaped over the ridge for the final time and sped out over the ocean beyond. The pilot aligned the nose of his helicopter onto its new course, checking the display Death Song had brought onto the HSD.

Satisfied they had the correct heading, he shoved the column forward, and the MH-60K slashed through the night toward Guam.

C H A P T E R

21

Captain Edmonton awoke with a start, immediately aware of the painful throbbing in his hand. A wave of dread washed over him as he remembered where he was; he leaned back in the darkness, becoming aware of the scratching that had invaded his sleep and awakened him. *An animal of some kind?* he wondered. A rat perhaps. He inspected the sleeping forms of the other prisoners around him for some sign of movement.

A crackling interrupted the noise, and a man swore softly across the cell. *Is it one of the prisoners trapped here with me?* Then Edmonton realized what he'd heard. Of course. Someone was trying to dig his way out of the cell.

That's what you should be doing, he chided himself, rising stiffly to his feet and wincing as his swollen hand grazed the wall behind him. He carefully picked his way across the floor, barely able to see in the dim light that filtered through the cracks in the thick door of the cell.

Perhaps things aren't as bad as I think, he told himself as he neared the man, who was obviously in the military judging from what was left of his uniform. The man's presence meant that someone must know the *Pleasure Run* had been captured and had come to rescue them. And the commotion in the halls an hour or so before the Japanese had quit questioning them likely meant an attack was being mounted by someone.

So if we could get out of this rabbit's warren, the captain thought, *we might be able to reach whoever's trying to rescue us.* He knelt down next to Garwood. "What are you up to?" he whispered. "Digging your way out?"

The sailor looked up. "Yeah. Trying to get out of this hellhole. These walls are just sand and gravel once the bamboo cover is pulled off. I think we could tunnel through to a passageway. It can't be more than a few feet at the most, here."

"But how do you propose to get out of this maze of tunnels even if you can get to one of them through here?"

"That's no problem," the sailor replied. "I know the way."

"You do?"

"Yeah, I've got a perfect sense of direction. And the Japanese have marked the way with characters on the support beams at each intersection, anyway. If I can get out of here, I can lead anyone that wants to come with me to the surface."

Edmonton said nothing, afraid to hope that the sailor knew what he was talking about.

"What can we do to help you, sailor?" Dan Brooks asked.

Garwood turned toward the prisoner from the

Pleasure Run. "Carry this loose bamboo over there and hide it behind those people so the guards can't see it if they come back in."

"How will you hide the opening you're digging?" Edmonton asked as Brooks collected the broken bits of bamboo.

"The door opens inward," Garwood answered, digging at the section of wall again. "When it's open, this hole will be behind it. But the trick is going to be not to dig through to the other side until this is large enough for us to get through. And it keeps caving in," he added as a tiny avalanche started around him.

Edmonton eyed the wall above the sailor. "That beam should keep the ceiling from falling on you at least. But I don't think any of the rest of this is going to stay put, as loose as this sand is."

"Yeah, it's going to take a while," the sailor agreed.

"Not if enough of us pitch in," another of the prisoners said, crawling toward the growing hole.

Petty Officer Morris checked his watch; there was no doubt in his mind, that something had happened to Johnson and the two sailors who had left their hideout. Morris turned toward Hopkins. "Something's happened to the three of them. Otherwise they would have been back by now. It's been six and a half hours."

Hopkins said nothing.

Morris leaned against the bulkhead and closed his eyes. "What I'd do for a drink of cold water."

All right, the petty officer thought to himself. Obviously Hopkins wasn't going to be any help, and Johnson had been the only one who knew where the food was hidden in the galley. That meant no food and no water if he stayed put.

And even if he left the sanctuary of their hiding place and somehow found food and water and safely returned without being seen, how would that improve things? Eventually they'd either run out of food or be found. He turned toward the sailor sitting across from him in the dim light, given off by an electric lantern that was slowly fading. "Look, Hopkins, we're going to have to get off this ship."

"You got to be kidding," the sailor said, clutching his rifle tightly in his fists. "We're safe here, man."

"Sooner or later we'll have to leave and look for something to eat. And then the soldiers roaming the passageways will kill us, just like they probably murdered your buddies."

"No way. I'm staying here and you can't make me leave," he added, his hand edging toward the trigger of his Kalashnikov.

"I'm not going to make you do anything," Morris said, holding out his hand, trying to calm the sailor down. "But our only choice is to leave and see if we can get to one of the launches off this ship and use it to head for safety. Guam isn't that far away—"

"You're crazy if you leave this room. We should wait. Someone will be here to rescue us."

"Yeah, but it could be days, and we'll die of thirst by then," Morris argued. "It must be a hundred and ten degrees in here now, and it's night-time outside. This tub is going to heat up tomorrow when the sun comes up."

"Go if you want, I'm staying."

Morris got to his feet, pocketing a full magazine of ammunition and then jamming a pair of boxes of loose cartridges into his combat vest. He glanced around, debated whether to take his helmet with him, and decided to leave it behind since it would only weigh him down. "I'm going. You sure you don't want to come along?"

Hopkins shook his head. Morris said nothing; he turned and carefully opened the hatch.

The four MH-60K helicopters circled Guam in the blackness, their slimes twinkling like stars. Oz received landing clearance from Andersen Air Force Base four hours after the Night Stalkers had left for their round trip to Kakira.

I can't believe we lost four good team members, Oz lamented, studying the lights dotting the island. Good men and friends; he would have to mourn them later after the hostages on the island were rescued.

The string of helicopters came in low and set down on the runway; moments after their touchdown, air force security personnel raced out and formed a perimeter around the aircraft, while Lieutenant Vasco and his marines whisked the prisoner from Kakira away into the night.

Oz unlatched his side door and a breeze whipped through the cockpit. He turned his attention to shutting down the helicopter.

22

Garwood swore under his breath as the sand crumbled in front of him and a beam of torch light from the passageway beyond cut through the darkness of the cell. He swallowed and then spun around to warn the others. "Is the guard outside the door still asleep?"

Brooks peered through a crack. "Yeah."

"It's only a matter of time before someone comes down this hall and sees the hole we've tunneled through the wall. We've got to go *now*. "

"I don't think you'll have to ask any of us twice," Captain Edmonton replied in a low voice. He turned toward those who had been helping clear the loose rubble that had formed the wall. The passengers and crewmen stood quietly, waiting to make a dash for freedom.

"You can't take her," one of them said quietly.

Edmonton turned to see Dan Brooks lifting the lifeless body of his wife.

"Captain," the crewman said, turning to Edmonton. "He can't take her, can he?"

"I'm not going without her," Brooks said evenly.

"Quiet down!" another of the passengers warned.

The captain turned to Brooks. "You can bring her along but don't expect us to stop and help you if you have trouble carrying her."

"I understand. I just can't leave her behind with these bastards."

"We've got to hurry!" Garwood warned.

"Okay," Edmonton said, picking up one of the crude slats they had removed from the wall. "Everyone pick up one of these sticks we dug out. They're not much of a weapon, but they might be useful if we meet any of our friends in the hallway." He turned back toward Garwood. "Lead the way, sailor."

Garwood stepped back and then threw himself headlong into what was left of the wall. It crumbled away, spilling him into the passage beyond in a riot of sand, pebbles, and dust. He rose, coughing and rubbing the dirt out of his eyes as Edmonton followed him into the passageway.

The captain blinked in the torch light, checking both directions to be sure no one had seen them. Without warning the guard who had been at the door of the cell came running around the corner of the passageway, his rifle held at the ready.

Edmonton struck out with the club he carried the same instant the trooper rounded the corner, the stick striking the Japanese in the temple so he fell to the sandy floor with a low moan. The officer stepped toward the fallen soldier and smacked him in the head a second and then a third time.

"Get his rifle," Edmonton said evenly, stepping back from the body. He turned and checked the hallway. Satisfied no one else had heard them, he looked at Garwood, who was still trying to get the dirt out of his eyes. "We need to hurry. It's just a matter of time until—"

"Right." Garwood nodded and then coughed. He blinked out the last of the dirt from his eyes and then studied the passageway. "Okay. I know where I am. We need to go this way."

"Are you sure?" Edmonton asked.

A grin flickered across Garwood's dirty face. "Trust me." He knelt and pulled a long-bladed knife from the sheath on the dead soldier's belt.

Edmonton grimaced and turned toward those coming through the opening into the passageway behind him. "You two collect the torches as we pass. If we leave this area in total darkness, it may take them longer to discover we're gone."

"Shouldn't we try to free some of the others?" one of the prisoners whispered.

"We can't chance it, and there're too many for us to all escape," Edmonton answered. "Your job is to get out so you can let the authorities know where the prisoners are; otherwise they'll never be able to find them in this maze of tunnels."

No one spoke, and Garwood turned and started down the passageway, making a right at the fork ahead of him without hesitating. The captain shook his head and hoped the sailor knew what he was doing. Then he eyed Brooks as he followed Garwood. How long can the man carry his wife before he breaks down? Edmonton wondered.

*   *   *

The four Americans stood around the prisoner who had been brought to Guam. The Japanese soldier sat in a metal office chair in the center of the brightly lit room, a burly MP on either side of him.

CIA agent Ralph Daniels turned away from the prisoner and glanced at the bare window; the blackness of the night made a dull mirror of the glass. After studying his reflection, which stared back at him with bags under its eyes and disheveled hair, he turned away. *I'm getting old,* he thought. No wonder they'd transfered him to Guam.

And ironically, now he was the man of the hour, in charge of getting secrets from a madman dressed in rags so the Delta troops who would arrive on Guam in a few hours could mount a rescue effort.

"Sir, he's fit for interrogation," the medic examining the prisoner told the agent, breaking Daniels's train of thought. "He'll have quite a shiner for a while where he got hit, but there doesn't seem to be any sign of a concussion or other serious damage."

"Good," Daniels said, crushing out his cigarette in the overflowing ashtray on the desk in front of him. "I want you to note in your medical report what the prisoner's injuries were *before* we interrogated him. We don't want any charges of brutality leveled at us later on."

"Yes, sir, I will."

"And you'd better hang around outside to give

him another medical checkup after the interrogation, so you can note that he suffered no injuries while he was in my custody."

"Yes, sir,"

"You can step outside now," Daniels told the medic, shaking another cigarette from the battered pack in his pocket. *Damn, I'd almost given up the coffin nails,* he thought wryly as the man left and closed the door behind himself. Nothing like a little trouble to bring back old habits.

But smoking was the least of his problems right now. He had five-hundred-some-odd Americans held who-knew-where; the latest fly-over of the island showed more bodies; and the cutter was apparently sunk in the harbor. The pressure was on to locate where the hostages were hidden on the island so the military could go in and rescue them before the madmen holding the island killed all of them.

Better start taping this, he reminded himself. He turned to the desk and snapped on the cassette recorder he'd brought with him, then picked up his lighter and lit his cigarette. He exhaled, studying the prisoner and noting the look on the old soldier's face. "You want a smoke," he asked in Japanese.

The prisoner nodded.

Now I know you understand Japanese, Daniels thought, happy that he'd been able to trick the man into reacting. The prisoner had refused to answer the air force linguist when the captive had first been brought in. The agent stepped forward and handed the wizened old man the pack along with his lighter, mindful that the soldier was probably dangerous. The agent noted that the two MPs standing on either side of the prisoner tensed up until Daniels had retreated a few feet.

Well, that's fine by me if they want to be extra careful, the agent thought. There was no telling how dangerous the little guy sitting in front of him was. He remembered a training film he'd seen at the company. During an actual interrogation, an innocent-looking woman had gone berserk and killed both of her interrogators, beating them to death with a chair while the video camera recorded the whole thing for posterity, forever enshrining the careless agents as examples of what not to do.

The Japanese soldier put the cigarette between his cracked lips, filter tip out, and tried unsuccessfully to activate the lighter.

Now that's weird, Daniels thought, closely scrutinizing the prisoner. "No," he said in Japanese. "Put the other end of the cigarette into your mouth." He watched as the soldier turned the cigarette around and finally got the lighter activated.

For a moment the agent wondered if there really could be something to the military's whacked-out idea that World War II-vintage soldiers were on the island. That was just too farfetched for the agent to believe. And yet this man didn't seem to know about filtered cigarettes or how a butane lighter worked. *Or maybe he's just a good actor.*

After scrutinizing the lighter carefully, the Japanese prisoner leaned toward the agent and handed it back. "So what's your name?" Daniels asked, exhaling a cloud of smoke.

The soldier inhaled deeply from the cigarette. "Shin Susumo, corporal in the Imperial Japanese Army."

Got him talking, the agent congratulated himself, suppressing a smile; what was often the hardest part of an interrogation was over. "This group you're with . . . When did it start up?"

Susumo shook his head.

"Started up the last couple of years, right? And what organization do you represent?"

Susumo laughed. "You Americans are always so transparent in your attempts to trick others. We both know we have been at war for half a century. You'd have to be a sorcerer to confuse me about that. You're not a sorcerer, are you?"

Now who's trying to trick whom? Daniels thought with the wisp of a smile. "No, that I'm not. Where are the prisoners you took from the passenger ship? Are they on the island?"

"I cannot tell you more, nor will I answer your questions. I have already humiliated myself by letting you capture me. Would you let me commit *seppuku?*"

"I'm afraid I can't have you go killing yourself just yet."

"I will not reveal any secrets that will harm my emperor."

"That would be Emperor Hirohito?"

Susumo nodded solemnly.

"You know he's dead, don't you?"

"He is not dead."

"Sure he is. He was just a figurehead anyway. Japan surrendered after we dropped—"

"Japan will never humiliate itself by surrendering. We will either prevail or die. There is no middle ground without dishonor."

This is getting nowhere, Daniels decided, tossing his cigarette on the floor and grinding it out. His hands shook as he turned toward the attache case resting on the desk behind him and carefully spun the twin locks on it to the correct combination. He unsnapped them and opened the lid to reveal a nearly empty interior with a black vinyl case, dubbed by the agency as the "Speak Easy."

The Speak Easy was to be used only in a dire emergency—and Daniels knew his interrogation would qualify as such. He unsnapped the case and spread it open, revealing a row of five pairs of plastic syringes, each filled with a variety of psychoactive medical formulas designed to make an interrogation subject speak more freely. His fingers touched the syringe of thiopental solution, then passed it up and settled on the new formula that had recently been fielded. The agent had heard some good things about the new drug which had simply been labeled "XTK"; now he would find out if it could live up to its reputation.

"Gentlemen," he said in English to the MPs on either side of the Japanese soldier. "This drug is designed to minimize inhibitions for a few minutes. It will not harm our prisoner in any way. I also want to remind you that the lives of hundreds of Americans are very likely at stake, so we don't have any time to waste talking to a prisoner who refuses to tell us what we want to know."

"Yes, sir," one of the guards said. "We understand. What do you want us to do?"

The agent removed the cover from the needle. "Just hold him still so I can administer it."

Before either of the guards could react, Susumo leaped out of his chair, whirling his booted foot forward as he spun, knocking Daniels backward. One MP quickly grabbed the prisoner and just as rapidly found himself flipped across Susumo's outstretched leg, facedown on the floor. Another quick movement by the Japanese soldier and the American was writhing on the floor, holding his groin.

The second MP grabbed Susumo by the arm and held on, skillfully thwarting the Japanese soldier's countermoves, keeping him secured in place. "Oh no you don't, you little SOB," the guard gasped. "Better hurry, Mr. Daniels. I don't know how long I can hold this jerk."

The CIA agent stepped over the guard who writhed on the floor, and jabbed the needle into a vein in Susumo's arm, quickly pumping the liquid in the syringe into it. Before he could withdraw the needle, the prisoner yelped like an animal and pulled away from his captor's wrestling hold, snapping the needle off in his skin as he broke free. He leaped onto the desk top, knocking off the recorder.

"Stop right there," Daniels yelled in Japanese. "We're not going to do anything to hurt you if you don't do anything stupid."

Susumo ignored the agent and dived at the window. The glass shattered, and the prisoner vanished into the night before Daniels could do anything to thwart his actions.

The agent ran across the room, his feet crunching through the broken glass, and gazed out to the pavement a story below. Then he turned back to the guards, who were now both on their feet. "He seems to be stunned. Go down and get him."

"Yes, sir."

Daniels turned back to the window as the MPs hurried out. The drug the agent had administered would slow Susumo down in a few minutes. Gazing out the opening, the agent realized Susumo was making no effort to run.

What's he up to? the American wondered. He watched with horror as the prisoner picked up one of the large shards of glass near him, knelt on the pavement, and rapidly slashed at his throat again and again, cutting his neck and hands to ribbons in the process.

The two MPs rushed out as Susumo fell into the pool of blood that collected around him.

Morris ducked behind an empty packing crate and hid in the darkness. The two Japanese guards paced past him, crossing the open rear deck of the *Pleasure Run.* The sailor waited until the pair had passed and then picked up a chunk of Styrofoam from the trash lying on the deck, hoping it would be capable of floating his rifle to the shore since he didn't relish the thought of reaching the island unarmed.

He worked quickly in the darkness, lashing the

rifle and its spare magazine to the plastic foam, using the laces he'd pulled from his shoes. For a moment he debated whether he should try to take his shoes or the boxes of ammunition along with him, then decided there was no convenient way to do so.

The sailor hid the small boxes and his shoes behind the crate that concealed him, lowered himself onto his stomach, and carefully slid under the rail of the fantail. *This is it,* he thought, taking a deep breath as he teetered on the edge of the deck.

Clutching the chunk of Styrofoam to his chest, he dropped into the ocean. Treading water, he wondered if the guards walking toward the other end of the ship would notice the splash that was only half obscured by the waves lapping at the side of the vessel. He floated in the pitch-black sea, wiping the water from his eyes and choking back the need to cough.

Morris waited a full minute to be sure no one was searching the water for him. Then he kicked off the side of the ship, heading for the shore, shoving the Styrofoam ahead of him as he swam.

23

Garwood double-checked the mark cut into the support beam in front of him. He couldn't afford to make a mistake now—the lives of the twelve people following him depended on it, and most likely the lives of everyone taken prisoner. He swallowed and then went on, now positive he was on the right track.

As the sailor came to another section of the living quarters, he slowed down, holding the knife he'd taken from the dead soldier. The quarters were now covered by bamboo and rice paper panels, many patched with bits of old clothing and leaves. *If just one person glances toward the screens and sees our shadows creeping by,* Garwood thought, *they can sound the alarm and we'll be sunk.*

He gritted his teeth and continued on, turning to observe those behind him. *They look like a bunch of scared sheep,* the sailor thought, noting how their wide eyes caught the torchlight. He wondered if they thought he was foolishly taking them farther into the dangerous prison. He turned away to check another of the beams. *Still on course.*

He slowed as they came to a winding, pitch-black tunnel unlit by torches; his prisoners bunched up behind him as he slowed his pace, cautiously treading into the darkness. He turned. "Give me a torch so I can see where I'm going."

Captain Edmonton pushed his way through the group and handed a sputtering torch to the sailor.

"Thanks," Garwood said, wondering how long the torch would continue to burn. *The trick,* he told himself, *will be getting out the front entrance.* It had been guarded, and they would have to deal with any soldiers there using only the rifle and knife taken from the guard and the improvised clubs and torches they'd taken. The sailor remembered the machine gun one of the guards had held and turned pale.

Just keep going and get them that far, he warned himself. *Deal with one problem at a time.* Maybe his good luck would hold out.

He slowed his pace and double-checked another beam. A new mark. Yes, he was certain they were getting close to the entrance. Just around the bend up ahead. He stopped and turned to those behind him. "Captain," he whispered to the ship's officer whose name he hadn't learned.

"What have you got?"

"The entrance is just ahead, and there were two guards there when they brought me in."

"Yeah, there were two there when I came in, too, now that you mention it."

"I'm thinking if we put out our torches and

walk out, they won't notice we're not some of their guys until we're right alongside them. We might be able to overpower them."

Edmonton didn't answer for a few seconds and then spoke. "I guess we don't have much choice. I'll pass the word along and have the guy with the rifle come up here with you."

"Sir, I don't think we want to fire that thing if we don't have to. Everyone within earshot—"

"Yeah, you're right. I'll have some of the stronger men with clubs come up here with you."

Morris crawled up the beach and knelt behind a large piece of driftwood, carefully untying his rifle and the spare magazine, which he jammed into a pocket of his wet pants. He rapidly walked across the beach into the foliage where he felt less exposed and sat down, his back against a palm tree. He caught his breath and tried to decide what to do next.

He had rested only a moment when the jungle around him seemed to grow quiet, leaving only a nearby cricket chirping a solo tune; then even the insect fell silent. Morris sat up, his rifle at the ready as he kept rock still, ignoring the tiny gnats that flitted around his eyes in the darkness.

A twig cracked to his right and he turned toward it. As he watched, he could barely discern the silhouette of a soldier, a bayonet and rifle held in front of him as he advanced.

For a moment Morris's finger tightened on the

trigger, and then he saw that the soldier was going to pass by him, apparently unaware of his presence.

Should I just let him pass? Morris wondered. No. The soldier must have seen him come up the beach. If he didn't find Morris, then he would spread the word, and more of the troops would come and search until they did find him.

Morris waited until the man was past him, then rose silently and smashed the butt of his rifle against the back of the man's neck. The soldier dropped with a low moan. Morris hesitated a moment as the soldier tried to get back to his feet; then the American brutally smashed the trooper's head.

The starlight at the mouth of the tunnel allowed Garwood to make out the silhouettes of the two guards ahead of him. As he approached them, one of the Japanese soldiers said something to him.

Garwood didn't know what to say or do.

The guard repeated himself, now standing erect as the group of Americans came to within a few yards of them.

"Mmmm," Garwood grunted and then broke into a charge toward the two guards, who were still unsure who they were dealing with.

The sailor's knife caught the closest guard in the chest, the force of the blow augmented by the running start Garwood had taken toward his foe. The blade buried itself to its crossguard, then snapped off as the soldier fell to the side with a groan.

Garwood hurled the grip of his broken weapon at the other guard, who jabbed at him with his bayonet, grazing the sailor's thigh. The sailor jumped aside and grasped the rifle, holding on with all his might as the Japanese soldier fought to free it.

"Kill the bastard," one of the prisoners cried, and then the Americans swirled over the remaining Japanese guard like a rising tide, pounding him with their clubs until he fell at their feet and the mob started stamping him.

"Kill him," the tourist repeated, kicking at the writhing soldier. Abruptly the soldier quit moving, but the throng continued to beat him, venting their fury.

"Stop," Garwood cried. "He's dead. We've got to move before the rest of them are on top of us." He turned toward the jungle and saw his way blocked by a tall figure that stepped out of the brush, rifle held at the ready.

"Garwood?" the figure asked. "Is that you?"

"Morris?"

"Who else?" the sailor said, stepping forward and slapping his friend on the shoulder. "You meet the damnedest people on this island. You know where you're headed?"

"Yeah, we're going to steal one of the launches that they've hidden on the dock down there."

"Look out!" one of the tourists cried.

Morris and Garwood ducked down as a Japanese soldier crashed out of the brush and fired his rifle.

Morris whirled toward the soldier and shot,

catching his enemy in a short burst that lit the night.

The island seemed to come to life with the noise. Japanese voices reverberated everywhere—behind them in the tunnel and ahead of them in the jungle.

"Cat's out of the bag now," Garwood hissed. He turned to the Americans behind him. "Come on. We're going to have to make a dash for it."

C H A P T E R

24

Captain Edmonton dropped to the rear of the escapees running headlong down the path in front of him and tried to help Dan Brooks, who had fallen behind. "You're going to have to leave her," the captain whispered to the man. "We'll never make it if you try to carry her. We've got a pack of them coming behind us, judging from the sound of it."

"No," Brooks said with some finality. "You go with the others. I've nothing to go back to now anyway." He rose to his feet, his dead wife in his arms, stepped off the path, and crashed into the foliage, vanishing into the gloom.

Edmonton stood dumbstruck for a moment and then, hearing the voices of the Japanese soldiers that pursued them, turned and sprinted after the others. Within a few minutes he had caught up with them, nearly stumbling on the winding trail along which Garwood led them. The trail abruptly sloped downward and then curved, leading them to a wooded section where he could hear the lapping of water.

This must be the dock I heard the sailor men-

tion. His eyes narrowed, and he recognized the shape of one of the launches from his ship. The two Coast Guard sailors were helping several of the women passengers onto it now while others in the group struggled to release the mooring cables. They aren't going to be able to get into the open sea in time, Edmonton realized, listening to the commotion of the Japanese who were coming closer. One volley of rifle fire would catch them all on the water.

The captain pushed his way through the mob scrambling aboard the launch and stopped in front of Morris. "Give me your rifle, sailor," Edmonton commanded.

"Why?" Morris demanded.

"You'll never get clear of this inlet unless someone holds the Japanese back."

"But you'll get—"

"There's no time to argue."

The sailor handed the rifle to the captain. "Here's the spare magazine," he added. "The safety's here," he pointed out, flipping the lever on the side of the Kalashnikov. "It's ready to fire now."

The motor on the launch coughed to life. "Good luck, sir," Morris said as Edmonton shoved them away from the dock with his foot.

He watched the boat bob away and then slash through the shallow water as its motor propelled it forward, nearly tossing one of the passengers out and bouncing on a wave. Its wake created a lapping at the side of the dock as the sea splashed up and down the narrow channel.

Edmonton turned and dropped to his knee on the crude wooden dock, covering the pathway with the muzzle of his firearm.

He heard a soldier's boots scrape along the path and spied the glint of the moonlight on the long spike bayonet of the lead soldier rounding the bend. Taking careful aim, Edmonton pumped the trigger once, downing the soldier with a blast that reverberated off the water behind him. "That's for the woman you killed last night, you bastards," he jeered.

A mass of soldiers spilled over the fallen trooper, and the American captain pulled the trigger again and again as quickly as he could, dropping each one that charged toward him. Five, ten, fifteen . . . It was impossible to count as the rifle jerked in his hands, wounding or killing one after another of the troops.

He pulled the trigger, and the hammer clicked on an empty chamber. Realizing he'd exhausted his ammunition, he ignored the soldiers rushing down the path toward him and jerked at the magazine in the rifle, unsure of how to release it. Finally he found the small lever at the rear of the magazine, and the metal box fell out. He jammed the spare magazine into the gun and rocked it back, locking it in place as the troops reached him. Frantically he jerked the charging lever back and released it.

A buttstock hit his temple, knocking him backward as his finger tightened on the trigger. The rifle discharged, downing the man who had struck him. The soldier tumbled over the American, who was immediately engulfed in a wall of Japanese soldiers.

*   *   *

Garwood looked back over Kakira as the launch distanced itself from the island in the darkness. "You think the captain made it?"

"No way," Morris answered. Both men were silent as the launch bounced on the waves through the night. "I didn't even know what his name was."

"Hey, they missed this," one of the sailors from the *Pleasure Run* yelled from the back of the launch.

Garwood turned toward the man, who was holding a black device that was impossible to identify in the dim light. "What is it?" Garwood hollered over the noise of the motor running full out.

"An emergency beacon. Stuffed in the compartment behind some rags. Should I activate it?"

"I don't know," Morris answered. "What about the soldiers on the island? Could they home in on it?"

"I never saw them with any radio equipment," Garwood told the petty officer.

"They used messengers all the time they questioned me," one of the tourists said, nursing his broken arm.

Morris thought a moment. "Activate it."

"I'm afraid the Japanese soldier you brought in didn't provide us with much information before he killed himself," Agent Daniels informed Oz, who glanced at the men ringing the conference table. Air Force Ensign Addis, the three other Night Stalkers pilots, and Lieutenant Leroy "Sudden" Tomlin, head of the Delta Forces team that had arrived at Guam, all sat glumly silent.

Finally Sudden spoke. "So what you're saying is

that we're like an atheist at his own funeral; all dressed up with no place to go."

"That's about it," Daniels agreed, tapping another cigarette from a new box he'd retrieved from his jacket.

"Is there anything from the fly-overs that might suggest where the hostages are?" Oz asked the Air Force ensign.

"We can see a lot of activity on the south end of the island," Addis answered. "And we've tried every trick in the book, from infrared to computer enhancement. But there's nothing to confirm that the hostages are on the south side—or even on the island."

"Could they still be on the ship?" one of the Night Stalker pilots asked.

"Not many of them," Addis answered. "Our fly-bys show a lot of people and equipment leaving *Pleasure Run* and then coming back to her empty. We're pretty sure they're all on the island."

"It would make sense if they were on the south side," Oz nodded, studying one of the new photos in front of him on the table. "If the hostages were at that end of the island, then their captors wouldn't have to haul them clear across Kakira."

"But surely there'd be some sign of more than five hundred hostages," Sudden protested. "The island is so small. I can't see how they'd hide them without our being able—"

"We think they may have an extensive network of tunnels on the island," Addis interrupted. "I have a series of photos that show twenty-four soldiers marching right into this opening right here. And there appear to be two more—here and here."

"If they really have been there since World War II," Daniels said, "they could have some real serious fortifications built on that island. Nothing I heard from the prisoner you brought me indicated that he couldn't have been on that island all that time. His clothing was homemade but was modeled off the old Japanese military uniform, and he claimed to be at war with us still."

"And he was definitely into ritual suicide," Sudden added, causing the CIA agent to blush.

"Well, if we don't know where they are," Oz said, pushing back his chair and tapping the photos in front of him into a neat pile, "I think we'd better wait for the navy task force to get there. The Japanese were notorious for mistreating and killing their prisoners during the war. If we go charging in there without knowing what we're looking for we'll likely get the prisoners killed and get ourselves shot up to boot. I can't see risking it. How do you feel, Sudden?"

The black officer tapped the table with his pencil and then looked Oz in the eyes. "I concur."

"It's five A.M.," Oz said. "I think it's time to call it a—"

He was interrupted by a navy ensign who burst through the door of the conference room. "Captain Carson," the newcomer said, approaching Oz and saluting. "Sorry to intrude, but we thought you'd better see this right away."

"What have you got?" The airman stood and took the sheet, quickly reading it as the other men in the room waited silently. "Gentlemen, this may be the break we needed." Oz handed the paper to

Sudden. "An emergency beacon has been received, and triangulation places it near Kakira, moving this way. The beacon appears to be of the type that the *Pleasure Run* had on its launches and life rafts."

"A trick?" Daniels asked.

"Could be," Oz answered. "But something tells me it isn't. Addis, let's see if the air force can scramble a plane for a quick look-see. While they're doing that, I'm going to take a chopper out there so we can be ready if there's anyone to pick up. If somebody has managed to escape from the island, that might be just the break we're looking for."

Major Yoshiro Tashida scowled at the American captain whom his men forced to kneel in front of him. The Japanese officer pulled his *katana* from its sheath, the blade ringing in the silence of the underground room, his men standing breathlessly at the sight of the magnificent blade.

"This man has disgraced our *dôzoku* and must be made an example of," Tashida told the officers gathered around the walls of the room. "We will not be put to shame by an inferior race."

The major looked each man in the eye and then resumed his inspection of the American. "Tell him he is to die," Tashida ordered his translator, glaring at the American, waiting to see what the troublemaker's reaction to his edict would be.

When the translator finished, Edmonton looked Tashida in the eye. "Go sit on your thumb, you stupid baboon."

"What did he say?" the major asked.

Private Kuroshima swallowed and then spoke. "It is nothing, major. He merely taunts you."

"What did he say?" Tashida roared.

"He said . . . That you should sit on your thumb . . . a sexual slur, I think."

"Is that all?"

"And that you were a baboon."

Tashida spread his legs slightly, raising his sword. The American refused to flinch. The major yelled as he brought the *katana* slicing sideways through the air, its blade singing as it fell across the American captain's neck, severing his head. Edmonton's body flopped backward and his head rolled across the sandy floor.

The major carefully wiped his blade on Edmonton's uniform and then turned to Lieutenant Ishimoto. "Put his head on a stick and take it to each of the cells where the remaining Americans are. Have Kuroshima tell each group that this is what will happen to anyone else who tries to escape."

"*Hai,*" the soldier said, scooping up the head and leaving the room with the translator.

Tashida resheathed his sword and turned toward the rest of his officers. "Tomorrow the Americans will come. Tonight's attack was only a test to see how well we would do. We did well, but still they will come. When they come, our first duty will be to kill the prisoners. Then we will defend the island to the death if we must."

"*Hai,*" the officers said, saluting as the major swaggered from the room.

25

The east glowed in bright pinks as the MH-60K helicopter raced across the gently heaving ocean. "We're right on the money for a direct course to the beacon," Death Song announced.

"All right, gang," Oz said over the intercom, "let's stay sharp. They should be down here somewhere." The pilot's tired eyes scanned the sea in front of him; the deep water seemed to hold the night in its dark depths while the surface rippled with the scarlet and purple of the rising sun. High above the water, wisps of thin white clouds glowed in the Pacific light.

"I think I see something at nine o'clock," Oz told his crew. "I'm taking us off course to check." He kicked his left rudder pedal and eased back on the control column to reduce their speed.

"That looks like it," Death Song agreed, inspecting his directional display. "Yeah, that's the source of the emergency beacon."

Oz pulled back on the column to reduce their speed further, mindful that the boat ahead of him might be a trap and the helicopter might come under attack. But his fears were allayed as the helicopter neared the launch; it was jammed with waving tourists and sailors. "Do you see any weapons among them, Death Song?" the pilot asked, throwing his chopper into a tree-topper that circled the boat, keeping the nose of the helicopter facing the vessel.

"They look unarmed to me," the navigator answered. "They're cutting their engine."

Oz brought the control column to its center position and slowed the MH-60K into a hover above the launch, which bounced in the low waves. He carefully lowered the collective pitch lever, dropping the aircraft closer to the water, close enough to reach those below with the winch. "O.T. and Luger, prepare to bring them onboard. We can't wait for them to take the launch all the way to Guam. We need to learn what they know right away."

"Yes, sir," O.T.'s voice answered.

The pilot toggled his radio on. "This is NS-1 calling Andersen Air Force Base. Come in please."

The radio crackled in his headphones. "NS-1, this is Andersen. Go ahead."

"We've reached the site of the emergency beacon and have found what appear to be passengers and crewmen from the *Pleasure Run*. We're picking them up now to bring them directly back to the base."

"Do you need help in ferrying them, NS-1?"

"Negative. We can get them all aboard. I do want my people and the Delta Force detachment on alert. These people may have the information we need. Over."

"We read you, NS-1. We will relay your orders."

"Thanks, Andersen. Over and out."

O.T. slid open the side door and waved at the cheering passengers in the launch below him. "Okay," the warrant officer said over his intercom. "Hold it right there and we'll be in good shape, Captain. I'm not sure I need to go down to secure them to the cable—it looks like they have some sailors on board down there who could handle the harness."

"All right, let's see if they can manage it," Oz replied. "Can you take the winch controls back there? I can't see what's going on from here."

"I've got the winch controls."

"I'll guide it down," Luger reported from the door, preparing to use hand signals to let O.T. know when to turn the winch motor on and off.

"I'm lowering now," the warrant officer told the aircrew. The motor above the door purred to life, and the cable and its harness dropped toward the applauding passengers in the launch below.

Major Tashida stepped through the *torii*, the wooden gate that marked the *jinja* where he and his men had built a shrine to their gods. Here he had offered gifts of cakes and flowers to the *kami* during the island's religious ceremonies, the *matsuri*, which he led. Now the cooking fires from the openings in the tunnels left a thin cloud of smoke, which hung over the hillside as the sun rose above the tall cliff behind him, warming his jacket with its light.

He knelt in front of the holy pole decorated with sacred objects: folded *gohei* papers, strands of hemp, strips of cloth. Tashida placed his *gohei* on the shrine and prepared to pray to the deity that stayed in the shrine at all times.

Today I must pray long and fervently, he told himself. With their abilities to see at night, he had little doubt that the Americans would return with the darkness. *Tonight they will come. Let us be ready for them.*

"Wait a minute," Agent Daniels said, shifting in his chair as he interviewed two of the former captives in the conference room. "You're telling us that you know *exactly* where the hostages are being kept in that maze of tunnels that you say runs all over the island?"

"Yes, sir," Garwood nodded, his eyes darting toward the soldiers sitting around the table. "I don't know what you call it, but I can always find my way back if I pay attention to the path I've taken. I never get lost on land."

"I can vouch for that," Petty Officer Morris agreed, leaning forward in his chair next to the sailor. "Garwood took us right to the dock where the Japanese had hidden the boats."

"Could you draw us a map that would get us to the hostages?" Oz asked.

"Yes, sir, I know I could."

Sudden glanced at Oz, then spoke. "If we had a

map, we'd stand a good chance of getting there before the Japanese knew they were under attack—especially if they're sending messages back and forth by runners like the hostages say they are."

"Sir, there's something else you should know," Morris said. "The *Pleasure Run* apparently was smuggling some military equipment."

"SLMs?" Oz asked.

"What are those?" Daniels interrupted.

"Shoulder-launched missiles," Morris answered. "Yes, sir, the crewmen that I hid with on the *Pleasure Run* said they had opened ten crates with six missiles each, and they thought there could have been an additional dozen or more containers aboard that they didn't have time to uncrate. The Japanese used the missiles to knock out our cutter."

"And down two of my helicopters," Oz added grimly. "What else did they have on board?"

"The crewmen weren't sure. But they did have rifles and a lot of ammunition. Possibly scores of AKs. And whatever they've stripped from our cutter."

"So our Japanese friends have some very modern equipment along with their vintage rifles and machine guns," Daniels said. "That really complicates matters. Captain Carson and Lieutenant Tomlin, I think you should wait for the task force to handle this."

Oz turned toward Morris and Garwood. "How are they treating the prisoners?"

"Horribly," Garwood answered.

"That's true," Morris agreed. "They're torturing

most of them, eventually killing them. You can't wait around, sir."

"If I were still on that island," Garwood said, "I would rather take my chances with a quick rescue than wait around and be killed little by little."

"That's not all," Sudden added. "During World War Two, the Japanese regularly killed their prisoners as well as themselves when it looked like capture was imminent. These people seem to be still abiding by the warrior code that dominated their culture during that period. So the task force may have the firepower to hit the island hard and overcome the Japanese with sheer force—"

"But that will be cold comfort if the hostages are all killed," Morris finished.

"We could get in there quick and rescue the hostages before they even knew what had hit them," Sudden said.

"But how are you going to get several hundred hostages off the island?" Daniels objected.

Ensign Addis cleared his throat and then spoke. "We might be able to distract them with an air strike on the far side of the island. That could be handled from here if Washington gave us the go-ahead."

Oz turned toward the air force ensign. "Do you know how many Sea Stallions the navy has at the base here?"

"I'm not positive."

"Ballpark figure," Oz pressed.

"I think around a dozen."

"Those helicopters are rated for thirty-eight passengers," Oz said. "But we could squeeze forty or even forty-five for a quick short hop."

"That still would leave you with forty-some hostages," Daniels said.

"I don't think so," Garwood argued. "The Japanese have killed at least that many in the fight to take the ships and afterward in torturing the prisoners."

"Mercy," Daniels said, blanching.

"We could carry the hostages out to the *Pleasure Run* here in the harbor," Sudden suggested, tapping a photo on the table in front of him. "Morris says there's just a small contingent on the ship. We could overpower or at least contain them while we transfered some of the hostages to the ship, and then the air force could pound the island."

"Garwood?" Oz said.

"Sir?"

"I want you to get started on that map."

"I'd like to go along."

Oz thought it over. "Okay, but make the map, too, just in case Washington doesn't approve." The pilot turned to the air force officer sitting at the table. "Ensign Addis, check and see how many fighter bombers and Sea Stallions the air force and navy can bring into play if we need them."

"Yes, sir."

"Sudden," Oz continued. "I'm going to contact Commander Warner to see what Washington wants us to do. It's hard to say which way Washington will go, but I have a feeling we'll get a green light for a rescue mission."

Thirty minutes later, Oz had orders from Washington to commence a rescue effort as soon as it was practical; the Joint Chiefs of Staff issued orders that cut through the red tape between the services, combining the assets of Andersen air base and the Agana Naval Air Station.

By noon, the four Night Stalkers pilots, Sudden, and Ensign Addis had formulated a detailed plan that would take them to the island, coordinating their raid on the tunnels at the south with diversionary air strikes by the Guam-based contingent of the air force. The air strikes would first hit the north and center of the island, then the entire island once the hostages had been removed.

"It looks good," Sudden said after they'd gone over the plans one final time.

"I wish we had the luxury to go in at night," one of the Night Stalkers remarked.

"Me, too," Oz agreed. "But Washington wants those people out ASAP, and we don't have much choice in the matter. We can go in with the sun to our backs, though. Coupled with the air strikes, I think that should keep them confused enough to get you in without too great a problem. The next catch will be keeping the Japanese from harming the hostages whom we can't immediately transport back in the Sea Stallions."

"I think the air power we can call in should handle that," Sudden said.

"I hope so."

Both men sat silent for a moment, and then the pilot spoke. "I can't see anything else we need to hash out. Let's brief our men."

"Yes, sir."

* * *

On Kakira, Dan Brooks pulled another handful of sand over the shallow grave he'd dug. "You deserved better, Mary," he whispered, wiping his eyes and choking back a sob.

Crouching to avoid detection, he carefully pulled a dead limb over the grave so it wouldn't be found, then crept toward a bush that was large enough to hide him. Still in a crouch, he studied the jungle around him and then left the gravesite.

Now the hunted becomes the hunter, Brooks told himself. The Japanese were going to pay for killing his wife. Brooks vowed to take as many of them as he could before they found and killed him.

26

The sun was setting as the four Night Stalkers helicopter pilots hauled their aircraft into a tight, giddy turn that brought them onto a new course heading approaching Kakira with the sun at their backs. Though the approach was not as secure as going in during the night, it would still make it very hard for observers on the ground to spot them until they were almost on top of the island.

"Avenging Storm One, you have a go-ahead to complete the mission," Warner informed Oz via satellite link. "Proceed to your objective. I have word that the air force is on schedule, too."

"Thanks, Avenging Mother," the pilot replied to his commander. "We will contact you later. Over and out." Oz switched to his air battle net UHF channel and spoke to the three MH-60Ks flying in single line behind him as well as the twelve navy transports that tagged five kilometers behind the army aircraft. "This is AS One. We're proceeding according to plan. Arm your weapons but hold your fire as long as possible; the clock starts when the shooting does; we want the Delta Forces to have maximum time to get their job done. Let's drop to nap-of-the-earth flight *now*. Over and out."

Oz engaged his terrain following/terrain avoidance autopilot that would drop the helicopter to minimum altitude, using its short-range radar to determine accurately the distance above the waves. "Arm our weapons. Death Song, give me the rocket and machine-gun pods. You take the Hellfires."

"That's a roger."

"We're powered up back here in the gunner's compartment." O.T.'s voice crackled on the intercom.

"There's the island," Death Song announced, nodding toward the speck that appeared at the edge of the horizon, partially shrouded in a low cloud. "ETA ten minutes—right according to schedule."

"Sudden," Oz said over the intercom, "we're ten minutes away."

"We're running on nervous energy back here already," the officer answered. "We're ready to do our thing."

Oz watched the island grow ahead of them while the waves rolled beneath, stirred up by the reefs lying under the surface. "There's the *Pleasure Run* dead ahead of us." Within seconds they were almost on top of the ship, the helicopter's shadow reaching the vessel before the helicopter and dancing momentarily across its stern before they hurtled past. "AS One to Sea Stallion One," the pilot called on his radio.

"We read you, AS One," the pilot of the Sea

Stallion called from far behind the army helicopters.

"The decks of the *Pleasure Run* look clear. We didn't see anyone on them when we passed. Looks like it will be ready for a fallback position if we need one for the hostages."

"I'll relay the news to Lieutenant Vasco."

"AS One, over and out," Oz said, clicking off his radio. "Heads up, everyone; we're headed in," he warned his crew.

The helicopter raced above the waves that piled up in the shallows and crashed onto the sandy beach, kicked to the east by gusts of wind. Abruptly the tranquil scene was broken as a hail of bullets pelted the side of the MH-60K and pocked the windscreen.

"They've spotted us," Oz announced over both the radio and intercom. "Fire at will."

For a moment, the weapons on the helicopters chasing toward the beach were quiet. But as they crossed above the beach and rose in a reeling climb over the jungle, the door gunners spotted targets and their Miniguns blazed, throwing fire and lead in thunderous bursts.

"Machine-gun nest at one o'clock," Death Song yelled over the din.

"I've got it," Oz answered. He shoved his chopper slightly off course, and tapped the button on his control column, expertly sending a 70-mm rocket from its pod. The pilot immediately brought his aircraft back on course, and the MH-60K raced past the position moments after the rocket blew the gun and its crew apart in a fiery explosion.

"There's the SP," Death Song said.

"I see it," Oz replied, clicking on his radio. "We're starting the run for the LZ. Four, you hang back and give us air support until all our dogs are off."

"That's a roger, One."

"You're X-ing our LZ," Death Song told the pilot, another long burst from the side guns nearly overwhelming his voice.

The low peaks of Kakira ahead of them were suddenly lit by flame, as if the sun were rising in the north. "Looks like the air force is right on schedule," Oz said, half to himself. He ignored the smoke clouds and fire that continued to blaze into the evening sky, knowing that the napalm and bombs would be taking a heavy toll of the Japanese troops at the north and center of the island.

"We're headed in," the pilot announced, dropping his collective pitch lever so fast he seemed to float in his seat, the helicopter dropping earthward in a near fall. The thumping rotors raised a cloud of sand and air that lifted them upward, cushioning their descent toward the ground. Oz depressed the collective further, bringing the helicopter lower. The wheels rolled along the bumpy surface, and then the MH-60K came to a halt on the ground.

An explosion rocked the jungle to starboard, and Oz looked up to see AS Four beating past overhead, spitting rockets toward a position hidden from the ground.

Sudden and the rest of the Delta Force squad on board the helicopter leaped out and quickly ran toward the hidden tunnel that led to the hostages. As they charged up the hill, a Japanese machine gun opened up on them, cutting two of the soldiers down.

"O.T., can you see that machine gun at nine o'clock?" Oz called.

"Got it," the gunner answered, and his weapon blazed, chopping up the foliage around the enemy position and instantly silencing the weapon. Several of the American soldiers helped the wounded pair to their feet, and they resumed their charge toward the tunnel, one of the wounded men limping slightly as they were led to safety.

"Our passengers are clear," Luger called.

Oz lifted the collective, and the chopper leapt into the air like an angry insect. "Four, we'll take the overwatch so you can bring your dogs in."

"That's a roger, One."

Oz threw his chopper into a wide circle as the helicopter came in behind the other two that were now lifting off.

"SLM at twelve o'clock," Death Song warned.

The pilot swore under his breath, scanning the jungle and spotting the man standing in the clearing; Oz mashed the fire button on his machine-gun pod, throwing the control column to the side to walk the bullets toward the man holding the rocket launcher. Seeming to take forever, the bullets finally hit their target and the man tumbled over, the warhead exploding as one of the bullets struck it.

Sayonara, the pilot said to himself as the explosion ripped through the foliage. He turned his chopper away in search of other targets on the ground.

CHAPTER

27

Sudden fired his rifle, downing the last Japanese guard that blocked the entrance of the tunnel. "Go!" the American officer yelled to his point man, who went charging into the black opening, his M16 blazing as the bright flashlight mounted on the handguard of his rifle illuminated the Japanese soldiers hiding in the darkness.

Directly behind the soldier was Seaman Garwood, now dressed in army fatigues and carrying a carbine. Following him were four soldiers with M203 grenade launchers, with the rest of the soldiers in the squad tagging close behind.

"Get those light sticks down so we can find our way back out," Sudden ordered the soldier carrying a large bag of chemical lights. The private grabbed a handful of the tubes of glowing chemicals and dropped them along the tunnel, marking the pathway for their return to the surface.

Four explosions rumbled down the passageway as the grenadiers ahead of Sudden fired their weapons. One of them turned and shouted, "It's working, sir."

"Keep moving," the lieutenant ordered. *No*

time to talk, now. But a smile crept over his face all the same; no one had known if the grenades the launchers fired would be capable of bringing down the roof of a passageway. Now he knew they were. That meant they'd be able to seal off all the side passageways between the entrance and the prisoners, greatly simplifying their return. He jumped over the body of a dead Japanese soldier and continued forward.

There was a flurry of shooting ahead and the cry, "Medic!"

"Keep moving!" Sudden ordered his men, shoving his way forward with the medic following him. Stepping to his point man, who was kneeling on the floor, clutching a field bandage to the wound on his arm, the officer knelt next to the soldier. "Just sit tight," he said, watching the hallway ahead. "We'll be back for you in a minute."

"Yes, sir."

Sudden stood and took the point man's position, leading the other troopers forward. There was a flicker of movement, and then two figures were caught in the light of the flashlight mounted under the lieutenant's weapon. He fired at the two khaki-clad Japanese soldiers, who charged with their bayonets.

The American's bullets struck the lead soldier, who clutched his chest and stumbled. The lieutenant triggered another three-round burst that smashed into the other man's face, causing his head to explode.

Sudden ran forward, hurdling his fallen enemies. He pulled a grenade from his belt and jerked the pin from it. "Fire in the hole," he hollered, tossing the grenade into the chamber ahead of him where he had seen several enemy soldiers crouching.

The explosion shook the tunnel, knocking sand from the braces above him. He peeped around the corner and was gratified to see the room caved in, choked with rubble. Sudden shone his light across the chamber and was satisfied to see no movement. He turned toward Garwood, who now stood beside him, rifle at the ready. "How much farther?"

"Straight ahead. Look out!"

Sudden and Garwood fired at the same instant, cutting down the four armed guards running toward them. The American troops dashed forward a short distance to the intersection the men had come from, and the lieutenant threw another grenade down the opening from which the enemy soldiers had emerged. "Fire in the hole!"

The blast rocked the passageway and sealed off the branching tunnel. The soldier and the sailor ran down the tunnel, rifles at the ready.

"We're almost there," Garwood said, gasping for breath. "Here they are. All these cells—" The sailor tried to pry the nearest door open with his fingertips.

"Get down!" Sudden warned, pushing Garwood aside and firing. The soldier's shots were answered by a volley from the far end of the tunnel, sending bullets cracking past the two Americans.

Garwood dropped to the floor, sprawling face-down; Sudden fired another volley, pumping the trigger to send bursts toward the three Japanese guards who struggled to chamber rounds into their bolt-action rifles. Before they could return the Delta Force soldier's fire, the bullets from the M16 smashed into them, knocking them to the floor.

"Are you hurt?" Sudden asked, turning toward the American sailor lying prone on the floor.

Garwood rose to his hands and knees and spit sand from his mouth. "No, sir."

Sudden turned to the soldiers who'd advanced alongside him. "You two secure the end of the passage. Be careful; there're probably more enemy troops hidden down there." He turned to the engineer accompanying the group. "Bring that pry bar up here and see if you can open this door. It doesn't look like we'll need to use the C4."

The soldier put the sharp, flat end of the steel bar he carried into the crack between the door and frame and jimmied it open.

"Hey, lieutenant," Garwood called. "Most of these locks are just pegs."

"Open them!" Sudden ordered. "You three, help him."

Sudden followed his men as they unfastened the iron-plated doors leading to the prison cells, while other of his soldiers dashed forward, covering the hall with their M16s.

The lieutenant peered into one of the dark cells. "Come on out. We're American soldiers, here to take you home."

A weak cheer went up from the hostages, who crowded toward the door.

"Follow the glow-in-the-dark lights," Sudden told them, turning and pointing toward the green light sticks that gleamed softly on the sandy floor.

"We'll have helicopters to take you out shortly. Hurry. That's it, follow the light sticks," he told the woman who hesitantly stepped toward the entrance. "Just keep going."

"Can you believe all these people," one of the soldiers said as dozens of hostages filed past, rapidly making their way to the mouth of the tunnel.

"Check all the cells to be sure everyone's out," Sudden ordered the soldier. "When we leave, seal the tunnel off behind us with the C4 so it can't be used again."

Major Tashida stared over the valley, which had vanished in a sea of fire crashing over the bulwarks, trenches, and machine-gun nests, more of his soldiers vanishing before his eyes as he watched. He stood silent as the American jets streaked over the island again, dropping another flurry of napalm canisters that created a rolling conflagration to engulf more of the Japanese positions.

The major slowly turned toward his officers, a scowl on his face, simply gazing at them for several seconds before finally speaking. "Lieutenant Ishimoto, where are my messengers?"

"They are . . . They are gone, Major. You sent them down there."

The Japanese major's face became a mask. "Lieutenant Ishimoto, you take your platoon and go to the south. Your task is to kill the prisoners before the Americans come ashore."

"*Hai*," the officer replied, his eyes avoiding the major's. He pulled nervously at the strap holding the missile launcher he carried across his back and then turned, yelling to his men, who waited in the trenches along the hillside.

Tashida watched another pair of American jets drop bombs that thundered above the entrances of the tunnels along the northeast end of the island, hitting the openings with unbelievable precision. Then he turned and spoke to his remaining officers. "You will get every man you can find—it looks like a few of our soldiers have survived in the tunnels and are making their way back here now. And you will take these men to the south."

The major flinched as another series of bombs pounded the valley beyond him. "Corporal Ryutaru, you will get our tanks and head south as well. We'll see how well your maintenance has been over these years. We will prepare to repel the invaders when they come in from the sea."

"But, Major," Ryutaru protested, "the Americans are attacking the north. It is obvious they are clearing the way to land their men to the north."

"What is obvious is that this attack is a diversion. Otherwise they would hit the whole island to be sure they got every one of us. They are coming ashore to get the prisoners—those who escaped last night must have told them where we were keeping them. Now hurry, they are likely coming ashore even as you waste our time."

"*Hai*," the officers answered in unison, their eyes cast downward as another wave of fire swept over the northern shore of the island.

28

The four MH-60Ks circled the entrance of the tunnel like angry wasps, blasting anything that moved
outside the perimeter set up by the Delta Force
troops. Heavy blasts rocked Kakira as air force
bombers continued to rain bombs on the north and
central sections of the island.

"AS One to Sea Stallions," Oz called on the
radio. "Come on in to the LZ, the hostages are
ready to be picked up."

"We'll land one pair at a time," the lead pilot of
the CH-53D Sea Stallions replied. Two of the giant
choppers thundered over the approach, slowing to
drop toward the ground. Moments after they landed, their rear doors were lowered and the U.S.
Marines on board raced from the choppers, taking
up positions around the helicopters and reinforcing
the Delta Forces troops. Other marines dashed for
the entrance of the tunnel and quickly guided the
hostages toward the waiting helicopters, pausing to
help the injured and wounded.

O.T. swore over the intercom. "You're not
going to believe this," he said, "but we've got a

tank or something coming down the hill toward the tunnel. At eight o'clock."

Oz threw his helicopter into a tight turn. "This is AS One," he called on the radio. "We'll take the tank or whatever it is."

"It's all yours," one of the other pilots called.

"Two and Three, circle the tunnel," Oz ordered. "Four, drop back and guard the approach for the incoming choppers." He flipped off the radio. "Death Song, you take the vehicle on the ground with the Hellfire."

"I've got it," the copilot replied, moving his head so the FLIR image in his helmet monocle sent a pulse of laser light onto the ancient tank that belched blue smoke and rumbled with renewed energy toward the two Sea Stallions the hostages were boarding. "Hellfire is slaved to the target."

"Fire."

The navigator fired, and instantly the Hellfire on the pylon beside the MH-60K thundered to life. The missile tore away from the helicopter as the tank fired its cannon, narrowly missing the lead CH-53D parked on the ground. The gunner of the tank rotated its turret, readying for another shot at the chopper. But before he could fire again, the Hellfire reached the tank, striking at the juncture between the chassis and turret, ripping the machine apart with a furious blast.

"There's a second one coming down the hill behind the first," Oz warned.

The tank fired toward the Sea Stallions on the ground. The shell struck the fuselage of the lead chopper but failed to explode, passing out the other side instead and raising a huge plume of sand in the woods beyond the aircraft.

"Acquiring the second target," Death Song disclosed. A moment later, another of the laser-guided missiles chased after the invisible dot of light the navigator had focused on his target. Two seconds later, the tank detonated in a fiery explosion.

Oz circled the blazing wreckage, searching for other targets. His radio crackled. "Sea Stallion One is full to the gills and ready for takeoff."

"Head out, One," Oz answered. "How many does it look like you'll need to transfer to the *Pleasure Run*?"

"None, AS One," the pilot called back, his chopper rising in the air as Oz watched it. "Looks like at least a hundred of the prisoners were killed or are missing. We should be able to take them all back to Guam as we fill our choppers."

"All right. Take all your choppers directly to Guam."

"Roger, AS One."

"Sea Stallion Two, calling AS One."

"Go ahead, Two. What's the damage down there? How many were injured by the shell?"

"Only some cuts and bruises, from what my crew chief says," answered the pilot of the helicopter hit by the Japanese shell. "In one side and out the other, right above the heads of the passengers."

"Get out of there ASAP."

"We're headed out now."

Oz watched as the CH-53D lifted into the air and then circled, preparing to follow its sister ship back to Guam. "Sea Stallions Three and Four, come on in," he ordered the next two transports. "It looks clear."

"Hurry," Lieutenant Ishimoto ordered his troops as they jogged down the hill, their equipment clanking. Small-arms fire and several explosions had come from the area where the prisoners were quartered; the Americans were already attacking, just as Major Tashida had predicted.

The Americans have tricked us, the officer realized, slowing his pace and letting his men pass him. He hesitated for a moment, trying to decide whether he should send one of his soldiers back to contact Major Tashida or let them go on.

The major knows the attack is coming from this direction, he decided. *And more reinforcements should be here any minute.* Instead, he should try to down one of the choppers that was buzzing around overhead like a fly after carrion. He removed the tube from his back, remembering how easily he had downed one of the helicopters that had appeared the night before. He extended the launch tube, jerked out the arming pin, and raised the launcher to his shoulder, picking up Oz's MH-60K in the crosshairs of his sights as it approached him.

Before he could fire, his attention was distracted by the thumping of feet down the path behind him and a low, guttural growl. He turned toward the noise as the helicopter thundered overhead and shot past.

Ishimoto's mouth dropped open.

Dan Brooks charged toward the soldier, a bloody bayonet held like a knife in his hand as he closed with the officer. Ishimoto only had time to hold the launch tube in front of his chest, trying to block the lunge.

The blade grazed the slick surface of the fiberglass tube and then plunged into the officer's chest, creating a searing pain. Ishimoto fell to his knees in disbelief, the launcher dropping from his hands.

The American stepped back, ripping the blade from the officer's chest. Then he lunged forward, plunging the bayonet into the Japanese soldier again and yet again. Ishimoto's eyes glazed over and blood spilled from his mouth. He listened to the man's voice as the blade was thrust between his ribs once more.

The Japanese officer listened to the rhythm of the guttural words, even though he didn't understand them.

"That is for killing my wife." The bayonet sliced into the officer's flesh a final time and Ishimoto was dead, sprawled at the feet of the man he had considered an inferior captive.

29

Oz hauled the MH-60K into a tight climb over the palm-covered hill. "We've got a bunch of bad guys headed down from the north," he called to the other three Night Stalkers pilots, who were guarding the Sea Stallions as they took off. "And we've still got eight Stallions waiting to come in for more of the hostages. We've got to cut these clowns down before they can reach the LZ. Three and Four, you cover the east end of this section. Two and I will cover the west."

The four choppers wheeled across the sky, their machine guns blazing as they sighted Japanese troops rushing through the foliage below them, attempting to reach the spot where the hostages were climbing aboard the Sea Stallions. Oz threw his MH-60K onto a new path and fired three rockets, blasting the top of the cliff ahead of him where a Japanese machine gun crew was trying to set up their weapon to fire down on the hostages. The blasts ripped apart the rock; the soldiers dropped lifeless, riddled with shrapnel.

Oz pushed his chopper past the cliff and then dropped into a terrifying plunge back toward the beach, the Miniguns on either side of the chopper thundering as the gunners spotted enemy soldiers on the ground.

"Another of those tanks at two o'clock," Luger warned.

"I've got it," Death Song shouted a moment before he fired a Hellfire. The missile crossed the short distance and tore the tank open like an old tin can.

"We're taking hits from small arms," Death Song warned.

"I've got them," Luger yelled, "I can see where it's coming from." His Minigun blazed, and the slap of bullets against the underside of the helicopter ceased.

Oz spotted six soldiers charging out of the brush toward the LZ, firing AK47s at the Sea Stallion ahead of them; before Oz could react, the Japanese were cut down by the marines guarding the perimeter. The pilot continued on his course, passing the dead Japanese troopers, then circling back toward the jungle to watch for more of the enemy.

"AS One, Sea Stallions Three and Four are ready for takeoff."

"Get out of here, SS Three and Four," Oz called to them. "Five and Six, come on down."

"Stay back until the choppers land," Sudden warned the hostages behind him as the transports roared into the air. The tourists and sailors waited in a state of near panic, afraid they might not be able to board. The Army lieutenant watched until the next two giant aircraft came in and settled onto the ground. Then he turned toward the hostages. "Let's go!"

He and his men escorted the forty hostages in a mad dash from the tunnel, across the sandy path, to the clearing where the choppers waited for them. They ran toward the open rear hatch of the waiting CH-53D. As they neared it, a bullet passed through the crowd, miraculously missing everyone. Sudden stopped, his eyes searching the edge of the beach as he raised his rifle to his shoulder.

There, he told himself, aligning the front sight in the center of the rear peephole and firing a three-round burst. A Japanese soldier tumbled backward, his rifle flying over his head, a jagged .22-caliber hole in his face. Sudden verified that the hostages were nearly aboard the first chopper, then turned to face the tunnel entrance and signaled for his men to bring the second group toward the other waiting helicopter.

He checked the tree line and then swore loudly. He couldn't see it but he could hear it; the creaking could only be the treads of a tank. He swore again and pulled his radio from his belt as the hostages raced toward the waiting transport.

"We've got another tank," Sudden's voice called to Oz from the ground. "On the hill northeast of us."

"We'll get it," Oz assured him, booting a pedal to swing the helicopter toward the jungle. He studied the wooded area below him and then saw a palm crash to the earth and a tank come burrowing forward.

The pilot aligned the nose of his aircraft on the

target and fired a 70-mm rocket from its pod, then adjusted the bearing of his chopper and sent a second and third missile toward his target. The rockets streaked forward, two scoring hits on the turret and body of the rusty vehicle. The tank stopped dead in its tracks, and the commander threw the top hatch open and scrambled out of the burning tank. A moment later the ammunition inside exploded, shredding the tank to scrap and bowling the commander over.

"Anyone see any more of those tanks?" Oz called as he swung the chopper around in a half circle and then darted back toward the LZ.

"One, this is AS Three, we've got a huge contingent of troops and a few more tanks coming down the beach a mile east of the rescue site. They've got rockets—just about got us with one of them. Looks like they're trying to flank the LZ."

"I'll see if we can get the air force to help out," Oz said. "Pull back and watch for any sign of other troop movements." He clicked his radio to the air force frequency. "This is AS One calling any bombers. Could you place some napalm on the beach about a mile east of our LZ?"

"AS One," a voice crackled in the headset. "What's the target?"

"A mass of men and machines—don't think you can miss them."

"We're changing our course; headed your way now, just keep an east/west cordon open for us."

"We'll stay clear," Oz promised.

"One pass should do it; then we'll be out of your hair," the air force pilot replied. "Jeeze, they're right out in the open. We're starting our run . . . *now*!"

Oz turned the chopper to the north so they'd be well clear of the F-111 that came in low, its wings extended for maximum time over its target. Moments before it roared above the mass of Japanese troops charging down the beach, two canisters dropped from the plane, arcing toward the earth where they ruptured, tumbling and bathing the men, tanks, and earth with jellied petroleum. A moment later the liquid ignited, engulfing the area in a wall of fire that grew as the canisters continued to roll forward.

A second F-111 came behind the first and dropped its twin canisters in the area where a few scattered troops now ran toward the tree line, attempting to escape the wrath of the air force jet overtaking them. The Japanese troops were too late—the canisters fell in their midst. The conflagration engulfed them and they vanished in the flame.

"Holler if you need any more help, AS One," the air force pilot called as his plane wheeled out of sight around the west end of the island.

"That's a roger," Oz replied. "You saved the day."

"SS Five and Six loaded and ready to leave," a Sea Stallion called.

"Head home, Five and Six," Oz ordered. "Seven and Eight, come on in." *I'm beginning to feel like I'm working in Grand Central,* the pilot thought.

"This is Ground One to AS One," Sudden's voice called over the radio. "We should be able to get the rest of the hostages and the marines into the next two Sea Stallions."

"What happened to the rest of the prisoners?" Oz asked. "Are they being held somewhere else?"

"I'm afraid that's a negative," Sudden answered. "We discovered that several of the cells were piled high with dead hostages—most tortured and mutilated, from the look of it."

These animals killed at least two hundred unarmed civilians, Oz thought. "Get the choppers loaded and then we'll come in to pick you and your men up."

"That's a roger, One. Looks like we've pretty well cleaned out all but a few snipers."

"I just wish we knew where the head honcho of this bunch of butchers is," Oz said.

"I know what you mean," Sudden replied. "Chances are he's already dead."

"I hope so," Oz said, circling back over the beach that was now littered with the blackened corpses of Japanese soldiers. "AS Two, Three, and Four," he called. "Keep an eye on the beach. I'm going inland to be sure no more of the enemy are headed our way." The pilot eased his control column to the side and headed for the center of the island.

Major Tashida's cheeks were crimson as he sank to his knees in front of the *jinja*, bowing his head in shame. "Hachiman," he prayed, "I have failed you. I am *kegare.*"

He laid his sword and pistol beside the small shrine and pulled his jacket open, exposing his belly. He had no second to put him out of his torment once he committed *seppuku.* But so be it, he thought.

Perhaps the extra time of suffering would atone for his humiliation in the face of his despised enemy.

He tore the sleeve from his shirt and wrapped it tightly around the base of the sword blade, then grasped the covered blade, placing its exposed point against his belly. He hesitated a moment as he listened to what sounded like an approaching train.

Turning, he saw a helicopter rise above the cliff behind him, its blades ripping the prayer papers from the shrine and intruding into his private moment. With an oath, the Japanese officer threw down his sword and leaped to his feet, drawing his pistol.

These Americans won't even let me die in peace, he thought, scowling at the helicopter that hovered just a few yards in front of him.

"An officer looking for a way out of his troubles," Oz remarked, holding the helicopter in a hover in front of Tashida.

"A high-ranking officer," Death Song added. "See the braid on his hat and jacket. Think we could capture him?"

"No," Oz answered. "These guys never surrendered during World War II. Surrendering is a disgrace."

"And slaughtering innocent civilians isn't."

"Not if you're warped enough, I guess," Oz replied. He watched as the Japanese officer shook his fist at the Americans and then fired his pistol, its bullets harmlessly lodging in the Plexiglas windscreen in front of the two airmen. In a moment he had exhausted the ammunition in his Nambu; he hurled the empty pistol at the helicopter and then bent to pick up a rocket launcher.

Oz pulled the control column back, rocking his helicopter to the rear and putting fifty yards between him and the Japanese officer. Then he brought the helicopter into a hover as Tashida extended the launch tube and shouldered the missile.

"Say goodnight, Gracie," the American pilot muttered, nudging the control column forward to nose the chopper down at the same moment he hit the fire button for his rocket pod.

Three missiles streaked from the MH-60K and crashed into the earth, ripping apart the shrine and showering the aircraft with bits of sand and wood. The helicopter's blades rapidly dissipated the smoke to reveal the top of the hill, wiped clean of any signs of the Japanese major.

"AS One," Sudden's voice called, "all the hostages are clear, and we're ready for a ride out of here."

"Hang on, we're headed in now," Oz replied, his helicopter thundering over the ridge and dropping toward the beach. "Two, Three, and Four, how's everything look? Is it clear?"

"That's a big roger, One. We've pretty well cleaned their clocks."

"Let's head in then and get our Delta people. Time to boogie out of here."

Oz watched the widows of the two Apache pilots flinch as the final volley of rifle fire was launched toward the sky. The honor guard lowered their rifles, and the flags were removed from the coffins. Three minutes later, he and Commander Warner carried the folded flags to the two women.

"He served his country well and will be missed by all of us," the pilot said, his words sounding hollow to his ears. He swallowed and saluted. Then he turned smartly and marched back to his position while the bugle blew taps.

If things had been just a little different, Oz thought, *this would be my funeral.*

Only Oz would have had no family or wife to mourn for him, since Sandy had divorced him a year ago.

These two pilots died saving hundreds of hostages, and that means something, the pilot thought. He knew he would have forfeited his life if it had been necessary to save the civilians the Japanese had held. The two Night Stalkers had not died in vain.

He took his place alongside his men and stood at attention with them, proud to be one of the members of the elite helicopter team—proud to be one of the Night Stalkers.

Duncan Long is internationally recognized as a firearms expert and has had over twenty books published on that subject, as well as numerous magazine articles. In addition to his nonfiction writing, Long has written a science fiction novel, *Antigrav Unlimited*. He has an MA in music composition and has worked as a rock musician; he has spent nine years teaching in public schools. Duncan lives in eastern Kansas with his wife and two children.

HarperPaperbacks *By Mail*

NIGHT STALKERS *by Duncan Long*. TF160, an elite helicopter corps, is sent into the Caribbean to settle a sizzling private war.

NIGHT STALKERS—SHINING PATH *by Duncan Long*. The Night Stalkers help the struggling Peruvian government protect itself from terrorist attacks until America's Vice President is captured by the guerillas and all diplomatic tables are turned.

NIGHT STALKERS—GRIM REAPER *by Duncan Long*. This time TF160 must search the dead-cold Antarctic for a renegade nuclear submarine.

NIGHT STALKERS—DESERT WIND *by Duncan Long*. The hot sands of the Sahara blow red with centuries of blood. Night Stalkers are assigned to transport a prince safely across the terrorist-teeming hell.

TROPHY *by Julian Jay Savarin*. Handpicked pilots. A futuristic fighter plane. A searing thriller about the ultimate airborne confrontation.

STRIKE FIGHTERS—SUDDEN FURY *by Tom Willard* The Strike Fighters fly on the cutting edge of a desperate global mission—a searing military race to stop a fireball of terror.

STRIKE FIGHTERS—BOLD FORAGER *by Tom Willard*. Sacrette and his Strike Fighters battle for freedom in this heart-pounding, modern-day adventure.

STRIKE FIGHTERS: WAR CHARIOT *by Tom Willard*. Commander Sacrette finds himself deep in a bottomless pit of international death and destruction. Players in the world-wide game of terrorism emerge, using fear, shock and sex as weapons.

MORE ACTION AND ADVENTURE
8 ACTION-PACKED MILITARY ADVENTURES

These novels are sure to keep you on the edge of your seat. You won't be able to put them down.

Buy 4 or More and $ave. When you buy 4 or more books, the postage and handling is **FREE**. You'll get these novels delivered right to door with absolutely no charge for postage, shipping and handling.

Visa and MasterCard holders—call

1-800 331-3761

for fastest service!

MAIL TO: **Harper Collins Publishers**
P. O. Box 588, Dunmore, PA 18512-0588
Telephone: (800) 331-3761

Yes, please send me the action books I have checked:

- ☐ Night Stalkers (0-06-100061-2) $3.95
- ☐ Night Stalkers—Shining Path
  (0-06-100183-X) $3.95
- ☐ Night Stalkers—Grim Reaper
  (0-06-100078-2) $3.95
- ☐ Night Stalkers—Desert Wind
  (0-06-100139-2) $3.95
- ☐ Trophy (0-06-100104-X) $4.95
- ☐ Strike Fighters—Sudden Fury (0-06-100145-7) .. $3.95
- ☐ Strike Fighters—Bold Forager
  (0-06-100090-6) $3.95
- ☐ Strike Fighters: War Chariot (0-06-100107-4) $3.95

SUBTOTAL .... $_____

POSTAGE AND HANDLING* .... $_____

SALES TAX (NJ, NY, PA residents) .... $_____

TOTAL: $_____
(Remit in US funds, do not send cash.)

Name_____

Address_____

City_____

State_____Zip_____ Allow up to 6 weeks delivery. Prices subject to change.

*Add $1 postage/handling for up to 3 books...
FREE postage/handling if you buy 4 or more.

H0071